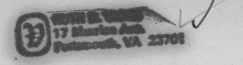

'You Can Cut Out the Pretence, Leon!'

She cast him a scornful glance. 'It must have been a strain to pretend you loved me!'

'Just what is this?' he demanded, and the arrogant tone only added fuel to her anger.

'I happened to overhear a conversation between your mother and sister. Now I know why you married me.' She broke off and laughed hysterically, out of control. 'You gave up the woman you loved and married me—all for this ring! You had no love for *me!*'

ANNE HAMPSON

currently makes her home in England, but this top romance author has travelled and lived all over the world. This variety of experience is reflected in her books, which present the ever-changing face of roman̄ce ̄ ̄ ̄ ̄ ̄ her-ever people fa̲

Dear Reader:

Silhouette Romances is an exciting new publishing venture. We will be presenting the very finest writers of contemporary romantic fiction as well as outstanding new talent in this field. It is our hope that our stories, our heroes and our heroines will give you, the reader, all you want from romantic fiction.

Also, *you* play an important part in our future plans for Silhouette Romances. We welcome any suggestions or comments on our books and I invite you to write to us at the address below.

So, enjoy this book and all the wonderful romances from Silhouette. They're for *you!*

Karen Solem
Editor-in-Chief
Silhouette Books
P.O. Box 769
New York, N.Y. 10019

ANNE HAMPSON
Man Without Honour

Silhouette Romance

Published by Silhouette Books New York

America's Publisher of Contemporary Romance

SILHOUETTE BOOKS, a Simon & Schuster Division of
GULF & WESTERN CORPORATION
1230 Avenue of the Americas, New York, N.Y. 10020

ISBN: 0-671-57136-2

First Silhouette Books printing March, 1982

10 9 8 7 6 5 4 3 2 1

Map by Tony Ferrara

America's Publisher of Contemporary Romance

Printed in the U.S.A.

Man Without Honour

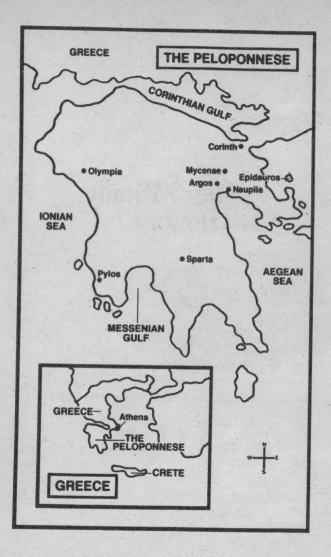

Chapter One

The garden had looked forlorn all winter. It appeared even worse when the first glimmerings of spring brought to light the few snowdrops and crocuses struggling to raise their heads above the dank tangle of weeds and long shoots of brambles which seemed intent on strangling anything that had the temerity to force its way into a world waiting eagerly for its appearance.

Kathryn Dalton stared out the window of her first-floor flat in the large country mansion and, as it was Saturday, decided to lend her aid to the valiant little flowers down there. After wrapping herself up in a coat and scarf, she found the gardening fork she used for her window boxes and went down the wide, balustraded staircase into the lofty hall of the beautiful house which had been converted into flats some years ago.

Each tenant was required to contribute towards the

upkeep of the gardens, but the man employed by the owner of the flats seemed to come only when the urge took him, which was not very often even during the summer months, and as the owner rarely visited the flats, this so-called gardener managed to get away with his neglect.

Each tenant would put in a few hours now and then, just to keep the gardens tidy, and Kathryn had done her share ever since she had taken possession of the flat on the death of her mother four years earlier, when Kathryn was only eighteen years of age. Her father had died several years previously, and as he had been an invalid for three years before that, he left his wife and daughter in pretty poor circumstances. Mrs. Dalton had managed to send Kathryn to a secretarial school, with the result that she now had an excellent post with a firm of wholesale clothiers.

'Hello, Kathryn. Surely you're not going out there already!' The cheery voice brought Kathryn round just as she was about to open the door. She grinned and glanced down at the fork in her hand.

'I must, Carole. The poor snowdrops and crocuses are being choked by the weeds that were left last year.'

'You make me feel guilty. Maybe I'll come out and give you a hand when I've done my washing.' Carole, like Kathryn, worked all week and did her chores on the week-end. She was on her own, though she had parents and several brothers and sisters. She had become fed up with the crowded house and had left home two years ago, and had been fortunate enough to get a charming ground-floor flat in what was one of the most desirable blocks in the area.

10

'You've no need to feel guilty.' Kathryn laughed, tossing the end of her scarf over her shoulder and bringing out a silken mass of russet-brown hair from beneath it. 'I just had an urge to see those spring flowers; they'll be a tonic after the horrible winter we've been through.'

'And it has been horrible.' Carole shuddered. 'I'd begun to feel I'd scream if that snow and hail and frost didn't come to an end soon!'

'Same here,' responded Kathryn grimly.

'The sun's coming through this morning, though, so I think I will join you in . . .' She glanced at her watch. 'In about half an hour. I'll just put my bedding and my smalls in the machine and then I'll be out.'

Kathryn was struggling with some obstinate brambles when Carole joined her less than half an hour later.

'Phew—It's harder work than I anticipated,' she exclaimed. 'But at least it keeps you warm. I feel all aglow!'

'You look it,' returned Carole with undisguised admiration in her voice. 'The picture of youthful health!'

'Thanks,' laughed Kathryn, her grey-green eyes dancing as she threw Carole a glance. 'But as a matter of fact, I feel about eighty! My back's killing me!'

It was Carole's turn to laugh. 'No wonder; you're going at it as if you've an overseer with a whip standing at your back. Take it easy, there's no urgency. The "little ladies white and green" won't mind waiting a while longer.'

Carole had a larger fork, and she began working on another bed altogether, going deep into the soil to uproot some dandelions that had had it all their own way since September of the previous year.

A sudden exclamation from Kathryn made her turn and cast her friend an interrogating glance. 'What is it?'

'I've found a buried treasure. Diamonds and sapphires! Aren't you envious?' There was laughter in Kathryn's voice as she held out the dirt-begrimed ring for Carole to take from her. 'Woolworth's, obviously. And a child's, I should say,' she added with a laugh.

'Yes,' agreed Carole, scraping some of the soil from it. 'A child's, judging by the size of it.' She handed it back, and Kathryn spent the next few seconds removing more of the caked soil from the ring.

'It isn't a child's. . . .' She had tried it on her little finger but found it slightly too large. 'It just fits my engagement finger,' she said, but took it off and was about to toss it away when something made her change her mind. 'It's ever so pretty,' she observed. 'Cleaned up, it could be a rather nice piece of costume jewellery.'

Carole shrugged her shoulders. She had been left some rather elegant pieces of jewellery by an aunt some years ago, and the superb quality of these had made her fall out altogether with the costume jewellery which other girls were in the habit of wearing.

'I'd not bother if I were you,' she advised. 'You've a couple of nice rings—that signet ring you wear, and your mother's engagement ring.'

Kathryn nodded, thinking that this ring, with its huge 'sapphire' surrounded by what could only be pieces of glass, was not really worth keeping. Again she was about to toss it away when something beyond her control made her put it in her coat pocket.

And as it was not a coat she wore regularly, the ring lay there forgotten until the following Saturday, when, glancing from her window to the plot where the snow-drops and crocuses were now flourishing in the sun-shine, Kathryn remembered the ring. After having her breakfast, she brought it out and scrubbed it with her nail brush.

'It's nice, no matter what Carole says,' she mur-mured, wriggling her finger to allow the stones to catch the light. 'I don't think I want to throw it away.'

She naturally began to wonder about the ring, be-cause now she was not sure it was as worthless as she and Carole had first concluded. For one thing, the setting was both exquisite and unusual.

Kathryn took it off her finger and dropped in into a little box where she kept buttons and the like, and promptly forgot it again until, three weeks later, she attended a week-end course at Branton Manor, an-other mansion about a quarter of a mile along the lovely tree-lined road in which she lived. There was another mansion farther along still, and one on the opposite side of the road. This one was occupied by an artist and his wife and was wholly a private residence, basking in the faded glory of its past. The one along from Branton Manor was flats, but its conversion had not been carried out with anything like the care and cost of the one in which Kathryn lived.

Branton Manor was now a college where one could attend seminars on varied and interesting subjects all the year round. Kathryn treated herself now and then, and this time she had been interested because the subject was local history. Most people stayed over in the accommodations provided, but those living within reasonable distance naturally went home each evening. The seminar began on Friday evening with a get-together in the hall over a cup of tea and a biscuit. After that the first lecture was given in what had—in its heyday—been the Blue Withdrawing-Room of Branton Manor.

Kathryn, sitting at the back, had a small pad before her on the desk, and as she listened, she made notes. This particular house had been owned by the Earl of Langley, while the one farther along had been built for his son and heir to bring his bride to on his marriage to a society beauty.

'Both mansions were spectacularly furnished,' the tutor went on. 'The owners were wealthy landowners but they came upon hard times and the inevitable result was that these houses eventually came on the market, but at a time when more like them were having to be abandoned in favour of smaller places. And so we have flats . . .' He spread his hands in a gesture of regret. 'And places like this, which most of you will know about if you're in the habit of attending these events regularly.'

Question time came, and Kathryn was ready with one or two queries about Thornbury Hall, where she herself lived.

'It was one of the many stately homes of the St. Clere family,' the tutor said. 'But they, like so many others, fell upon hard times, and one by one their ancestral homes had to be sold.'

'The St. Cleres,' murmured Kathryn almost to herself, and then, louder, so that all could hear her. 'They're a very old family, I think?'

The tutor, a middle-aged man whose whole life was steeped in history, nodded his head a little absently, as his attention was on the papers before him, which he was rapidly going through.

'They inherited the famous Penshurst around the mid-fifteenth century, having come into the property through an heiress, but lost it again when it was sold to the Duke of Bedford. The St. Cleres who lived in these parts were another branch, though, but equally as wealthy—in those days, that was.' He paused, having found what he was seeking for. 'As a matter of fact, I'm going to give one of tomorrow's lectures over entirely to the St. Cleres.' He looked at Kathryn and smiled. 'Have you some special reason for your interest?'

'Yes, I live in a flat at Thornbury Hall, just along the road here.'

A stir of interest followed this, and almost every head turned. Kathryn glanced down at her notebook, feeling embarrassed and wishing she had not mentioned living at Thornbury Hall.

However, the tutor knew it was now flats, and she heard him say, 'I believe the conversion there was tasteful—beautifully carried out by a man who was obviously not without money or ideas.'

'It is beautifully done,' agreed Kathryn, conscious now of a hint of envy on the faces turned towards her.

'I have a first-floor flat which looks across the grounds to the park and then to the hills.'

'Well, if you will bear with me this evening, I'll give you all the information you want tomorrow.'

Dinner in the large wainscoted dining-room followed the lecture, and afterwards the students from all the various seminars gathered in the lounge, where drinks could be bought. Large armchairs in blue upholstery were scattered about the massive room; small tables, stools, and settles were also there for the comfort and enjoyment of the students. Kathryn soon found herself drawn into a conversation with several other young people, women and men. The tutor, Professor James Marney, joined them, a tankard of beer in his hand. He asked Kathryn her name, seemed very interested in her, and soon told her more about the illustrious St. Clere family who, it was supposed, had come over from Normandy with William the Conqueror and fought with him at Hastings.

But it was the following morning before Kathryn heard the item of interest which sent her thoughts flying to the ring she had found in the garden at Thornbury Hall.

Dr. Marney had been reciting the history of the family, and his subject being local history, he naturally kept to the branch of the family which had eventually settled in Cheshire.

'There was an interesting story about some jewellery,' he said, glancing at his notes. 'Apparently there was a set of jewellery, a family heirloom—one of many, I suppose—consisting of a diamond-and-sapphire necklace, two bracelets, a tiara, earrings and other items. The craftsman who made this jewellery, a man called Sydney Abernon, was mad, so it was said. He had the "gift of curse," according to an old document which I once managed to peruse and which is now in the possession of another branch of the family.'

'The gift of curse?' someone repeated from the front row.

'Yes; he had the ability to put a curse on people.'

Laughter was heard, though subdued, from several of the younger students.

'Well . . . you may treat this with derision,' said the professor quietly, 'but this man, this superb craftsman who made jewellery for many European kings and queens, was feared greatly at that time, and it was believed that no one would be foolish enough to cross him.' Dr. Marney paused, flicking over a piece of paper in order to glance at the one beneath it. 'This man made a set of jewellery for one Sir Guy St. Clere, for the nobleman's wife, a woman with the reputation of being the greatest beauty of her day. When Sir Guy was told how much the jewellery was to cost him, he called the man a robber and refused to pay, offering him what, in his opinion, the jewellery was worth. Sydney Abernon had no alternative other than to accept, having already delivered the jewellery and had his request for its return arrogantly refused by Sir Guy. So he put a curse on the jewellery to the effect that if ever one piece became separated from the rest, the owner at the time would, along with his whole family, suffer the direst of misfortunes. The curse was to go on to all Sir

Guy's descendants and to anyone else who came into possession of the jewellery, and would come off only when the set was again complete.'

'It's an interesting story,' said one young student with some amusement, 'but not one to be taken seriously, I think.'

'Certainly not,' from a lady sitting at the end of the second row. 'One hears all sorts of stories if one delves into ancient documents pertaining to some of these old families. I am of course thinking of Nixon's prophecies.'

'Well,' said the professor mildly, 'we have to admit that Nixon's prophecies mostly turned out to be true.'

'They did?' The woman seemed puzzled by this piece of information.

'Many of them did, yes. One was of the way he himself would die. It came true, along with others concerning the family for whom he worked at Vale Royal Abbey in Cheshire.' No one had any comment to make, and the professor continued by saying that one of the pieces of jewellery had in fact been lost. 'I have never been able to find out what piece it was,' he went on, glancing down at his notes. 'It could have been any one of the pieces—a brooch perhaps, or a ring. It was said that it could have been stolen by one of the servants—one can never get the correct story when it happened so long ago. The interesting thing is that the curse seemed to be effective, as the whole family of this nobleman who owned the jewellery suffered in some way or another. The two young sons fought a duel to the death over nothing more important than a serving wench whom they both wanted. A daughter died of the plague less than a month later. The husband, mad with grief and blaming his wife for losing the piece of jewellery, made her enter a nunnery and he himself died soon afterwards, leaving a daughter, a child of five, to inherit all his houses and lands.'

'*And* the jewellery,' said someone from the middle of the room.

Another stir of interest had followed as the professor's narrative came to an end. Kathryn, her heart beating faster than normal, had several times opened her mouth to speak, to tell the professor about the ring she had found, but she had no opportunity of interrupting him. And now, when she did have the chance to speak, she was held back by some force quite beyond her control. A murmuring had begun, with people softly making derisive and sceptical remarks about the absurdity of curses. Someone asked the professor if he believed in this particular one. His reply was that he had an open mind, for while logic rejected the idea of one person being able to curse another, in this particular case the curse did seem to have been effective.

'Moreover,' he added after a pause during which he again consulted his notes, 'there is another story, of much later origin, giving an account of the disasters that befell the descendants of the child who was left an orphan. She herself married and had eight children, seven of whom died very young, either by illness or accident.'

'In those times the infant-mortality rate was incredibly high,' submitted a woman on Kathryn's right. 'You've only to go around an old churchyard to see how many died.'

Dr. Marney nodded his agreement but said nothing. Kathryn was still held back from mentioning the ring, but now her reticence no longer puzzled her. To mention that she had found a diamond-and-sapphire ring in the grounds of the house in which Guy St. Clere had lived would give rise to the kind of excitement which she would find far too embarrassing. She did say, however, when an opportunity presented itself, 'This set of jewellery was all of diamonds and sapphires—the whole of it?'

The professor nodded. 'Yes, it was, Miss Dalton.'

'It must have been worth a fortune,' someone interjected.

'It must.' The professor glanced at the man who had spoken. 'But I daresay those who inherited it didn't think so.'

'I wonder where it is now?'

'It's probably *all* split up.' The young girl who spoke added with a laugh, 'Curse or no curse, I'd not mind owning a necklace of sapphires and diamonds!'

Others added their comments before Dr. Marney, intimating that the time was up, brought the lecture to a close.

The following day, Sunday, the seminar broke up, but Kathryn decided to have a few words in private with Professor Marney. She found him in a small room to which she had been directed on asking at the desk in the hall where he would be found.

She told him about the ring. He was naturally amazed and asked her if he could see it.

'Of course. Would you like me to fetch it now—or

perhaps you'd call at my flat after you've finished here?'

'Yes, I think so,' he decided, telling her he had only to collect all his papers, make some notes for the college authority to retain, and then he would be free. 'I should be with you in an hour at the most,' he said finally.

Kathryn was showing him the ring a short while later, watching his face intently, wondering what she hoped to read from his expression.

'It's an extraordinary story,' he said, fingering the ring as though it were hot. 'It must have lain for many a long year, taking no real harm, and it's been disturbed by gardeners over and over again but never come to light until you found it.'

She said, taking it from him and putting it down on the table, 'What would you suggest I do with it, Dr. Marney?'

'It's yours by law,' he told her, smiling as she shook her head vehemently. 'You're afraid of it, maybe?'

'No, it isn't that. I don't believe the curse could affect me in any way at all. But I do think that there is someone somewhere who has more right to this ring than I.'

But the professor was shaking his head. 'The family definitely died out, Miss Dalton.'

'You can be sure—absolutely sure?'

'I've tried to trace some descendant . . .' He shook his head and added firmly, 'There are none of the St. Cleres left, I can assure you of that.'

'This other branch of the family,' she began. 'Surely they have a claim?'

'No, and if it were me, I wouldn't give it up to them. They're enormously wealthy, and in any case, in my opinion they do not have any right to this ring at all.'

But Kathryn felt it was her duty to contact the head of the St. Clere family, whose ancestral home was in Lincolnshire. She wrote a letter saying she had come into possession of an article of jewellery that might belong to them.

The reply came, and the following week-end found her showing the ring to Sir Algernon St. Clere, who immediately thrust it back at her and said, his voice rising to a pitch that was almost like a woman's, 'Take it away, girl! We don't want it! Off you go . . .' And to her amazement and disgust, he rang for his butler and within five minutes of entering the mansion she was being shown out.

'Well, that's that!' she exclaimed, putting the ring on her finger. 'To the devil with them! It's treasure trove and so it's mine! I shan't give it up to anyone now!'

Kathryn and her colleague were looking through holiday brochures during their lunch-hour break.

'I fancy Paris, but Jerry wants to go to Italy.' Averil Pagenham's voice was a trifle petulant. 'Aren't you glad you're single, Kate? You've no one to please but yourself.'

'That's true, but on the other hand it can be lonely, going on holiday on your own.'

'You never seem to mind, I've noticed.'

That was true. Kathryn always managed to find a way of enjoying her solitude when on holiday. She supposed it was partly owing to the keen interest she invariably took in things around her, especially if she was in a foreign country where the people and the cultures were so different from her own, to say nothing of the scenery and the pleasure of living in an hotel and having everything done for her.

'I've been thinking I'd like to try Greece this year,' she said, thumbing through the brochure she held. 'Either Athens or one of the islands.'

'My sister's been to several islands. She was very taken with the Peloponnese, though. There's a lot to see in the way of ancient sites.'

Yes, of course, reflected Kathryn. There was the famous Citadel of Mycenae, for one thing; she felt that that alone would be worth going for.

By the time she had returned to her desk after the lunch hour, Kathryn was all fixed for a holiday in the Peloponnese, having visited the travel agent, signed the form and paid her deposit.

Chapter Two

There was a cool and heady atmosphere about the gardens of the Hotel Hermes, situated on a promontory surrounded by the sea. Kathryn had chosen Nauplia as her headquarters because it made a convenient centre for visits to several archaeological sites besides that of Mycenae, which of course was to be the highlight of her holiday.

She had booked in at the hotel, then wandered from the grounds down to the waterfront, where the odours of fish and fruit mingled with the scent of the sea which penetrated deeply into the Gulf of Nauplia. She noticed a delightful *taverna* where seafood was a specialty and decided to try it for lunch one day. She walked beneath waving palm trees, delighted in the mountains that dominated the coastal plain, thrilled to that clear crystal air which, she had been told, is unique to

Greece, land of pagan gods, great philosophers and poets.

There were not many people about; the clerk at the travel agency had told her that, despite its wild beauty and all it had to offer in the way of ancient sites, this part of Greece had not yet succumbed to the onslaught of modern tourism. It was still the haunt of those who craved peace and relaxation away from the noise and crowds and a view of layer upon layer of concrete slabs relieved only by windows absurdly aslant to enable those behind them to glimpse the sea or mountains or whatever scenery the particular place had to offer. The Hotel Hermes was not a concrete block; on the contrary, it was low, and built with taste and a regard to what nature provided in the way of a setting. Trees had been left, even though it had meant building around them; a little rivulet was allowed its sparkling freedom instead of being culverted to provide more space. Pretty little bridges of rustic wood spanned this dancing stream which flowed into a lily pond before escaping at the other end to make its way to the sea.

The afternoon had flown; it seemed no time at all before Kathryn was again in her luxurious bedroom, taking a shower before preparing for dinner. She had bought three new evening gowns, a couple of full-length skirts and several glamorous tops, two of which were identical in style but one was knitted in silver thread and the other in gold. For her first evening she chose a white dress in cotton, very plain except for the silk cording that made a flower pattern on the front of the high-necked, tight-fitting bodice, and the flouncing on the bottom of the long, flowing skirt. A bracelet of plain gold, and the ring she had found, were her only pieces of jewellery. Yet as she entered the dining-room almost every head was turned. She knew she looked nice, that her russet-brown hair was lit with honey lights, that her eyes were happy, her figure supple and slim with curves which at this moment attracted the attention of many people, mostly men.

But it was the interest of one man in particular that affected her, a dark, clear-skinned Greek immaculately clad in a loose-fitting safari suit of white linen. The sole occupant of his table, he had seemed to catch a glimpse of something to her side, causing his dark, metallic eyes to widen in what seemed to be an expression of astounded disbelief. Kathryn felt her nerves tense as she wondered for one horrifying moment if her dress was torn, or tucked up in some way, but on glancing down swiftly she saw nothing amiss. As she proceeded to her table in the wake of a square-shouldered waiter, she was still wondering what had arrested the Greek's attention.

She had a table to herself, and as she sat down her eyes naturally sought him out. To her amazement, he had moved so that he faced her rather than having his back to her! She felt the colour rise in her cheeks and she picked up the menu quickly and held it in front of her face. But every few seconds she glanced at that table again; it was as if she had no control over her mind . . . or was it that he possessed some strange magnetism that drew her eyes to him all the time? The waiter appeared, but she was not ready and he went away again. She saw him go to that particular table and take the order. The wine waiter appeared, but the

Greek was still considering; the choosing of a wine was obviously of major importance to him.

After dinner there was a floor show, then dancing until midnight. Kathryn decided to watch the show and then go to bed. Somehow she was not even surprised to find herself seated next to the dark Greek. She had chairs vacant on both sides of her, and he took possession of one of them. She expected him to speak and was not disappointed.

'Are you here on holiday?' he asked, his eyes resting for a moment on the hand nearest to him—her left hand.

'Yes, I am,' she answered, some strange tremor of excitement rippling along her spine. The man interested her, seemed to hold her in some kind of suspended state where she waited, breathless, for something momentous to happen.

'You're staying here? At the Hermes?'

'Yes,' she said again, wondering why she did not resent the questions being put to her.

'Are you alone?'

She hesitated this time, her nerve-ends taut. But his glance was open, his lips curved in a half-smile, and she found herself answering, 'I'm alone, yes.'

'When did you arrive?'

'Only today.'

'How long will you be here?'

'Three weeks,' she replied. Then, feeling it was her turn to ask a question, she said, without giving him time to speak again, 'Are you staying here?'

There was the slightest hesitation before he said, his attention appearing to have strayed to a group of people looking around for seats, 'Yes, as a matter of fact, I am.'

'On holiday?'

He nodded his head. 'That's right.'

'What part of Greece do you come from?'

He looked at her in some amusement. 'My turn to be questioned, eh?'

'Well, I don't see why I should be cross-examined without putting the odd question myself,' she retorted.

'I'm on my own here; I'm not married, nor do I have any children to my knowledge,' he thought to add, amusement edging his voice. 'I can stay as long as I like, so I might just stay three weeks. Is there anything else which will be of interest to you, I wonder?' He still hadn't answered her last question, Kathryn realised. 'No, I don't think so, not at this stage, anyway.'

'At this stage?'

Kathryn looked questioningly at him.

'Forget it . . .' He took her hand, holding her fingers very much in the grand manner of a gallant in days gone by who was intending to kiss them. 'That's a pretty ring you're wearing,' he murmured. 'A most unusual setting. You're engaged?'

She shook her head. 'No, I'm not engaged.' And on noticing the faint inquiring life of his brows, she added, 'I wear it on this finger because it won't fit any other—except my little fingers, but it would slip off and I might lose it.' She gave him a smile, her eyes wide and honest, like a child's.

He still held her hand, retaining his hold when it did not seem in the least necessary to do so. She could not understand why she allowed this. All she did know was that the touch was pleasant, that the contact of flesh against flesh was sending absurd tremors racing along her spine.

'It's . . . pretty . . . isn't it?' she managed at last, and he nodded, still thoughtful. He released her hand.

'Very, and worth a lot of money. Where did you get it?'

'It's . . . er . . . been in the family for years . . .' She stopped, and stared, staggered by the lie she had never meant to tell.

'It has?' A long pause; and then, 'Would you sell it?'

She shook her head at once. She had never really considered it was hers to sell, despite her angry declaration to the contrary after being almost ordered off the premises of Algernon St. Clere. She still had the conviction—vague, it was true—that one day she might just run across the legal owner, in which event she would willingly give it back.

'No, I would never even consider selling it.' She paused and looked at him, wondering what he, a Greek, could want with it. Perhaps he was getting engaged and wanted something antique, and different. 'What makes you want to buy it?'

'I . . . collect antique jewellery,' came the response. Kathryn looked at him again, puzzled by the hesitation. 'That ring would make a most interesting addition to what I already have.'

She said, hoping to veer the subject from the ring she wore, 'Do men usually collect antiques? I mean, jewellery is associated with women, usually.'

'People collect all sorts of things these days, as investments.' His voice had a casual edge to it; he lifted one lean brown hand to suppress a yawn. 'Your stay here seems rather long,' he remarked, changing the subject. 'People usually spend no more than a couple of days and then move on to somewhere else.'

'Two days wouldn't be anywhere near enough for me,' she asserted. 'There's so much to see. I imagine one could spend a whole day at Mycenae for a start; then there's Epidaurus and Tiryns, and the Roman baths at Argos, and the ancient theatre . . .' She flicked a hand expressively. 'There's more than enough in these parts to occupy me for three weeks!'

The hint of a smile touched the handsome, classical lines of his face. 'What is your name?' he asked after a pause.

She frowned then, deciding it was time she made some protest against his questions. 'I don't think there is any need for me to give you my name,' she said stiffly.

'Only that I would like to know it,' he said in some amusement.

Kathryn felt at a loss, aware that she had no answer to this. She slanted him a glance, taking in facial qualities which were already impressed on her mind—the distinctive classical features of the Greek with those high cheekbones and rigid jawline. His mouth was thin yet in some indefinable way sensual; his eyes, the colour of harsh grey serpentine, were long-lashed and deep-set below finely marked brows. His olive skin was smooth and shiny. His raven hair waved a little; it was wiry and clean and greying at the temples. Kathryn judged his age to be around thirty-five, although he could be older—thirty-eight, perhaps. Certainly he had all the confidence and *savoir-vivre* of the mature aristo-crat, the noble qualities characteristic of those silent statues carved so many centuries ago by the pagans of Greece.

'I never give my name to strange men,' she said at last, aware that he was waiting for her to speak.

'I shall give you mine, then,' he said cooly. 'It's Leonides Coletis. I prefer Leon for short.' He leant back in his chair, totally at his ease. Anyone would think he had known her for months!

'Are you telling me to call you Leon?' she asked, nerves quivering as once again she felt excitement flooding over her, along with the expectancy that something was about to happen.

'That's right—but of course you'll have to tell me your name, won't you?'

She had to smile. His charm was devastating when he glanced at her like that, with the glint of amused satire in his eyes. She suddenly realised that she was acting in a manner completely alien to her—picking up a man like this at an hotel. Nevertheless, she found herself giving him her name, then heard it repeated. It rolled off his tongue in a way that made her catch her breath; his accent gave it an attractive richness which was exceedingly pleasing to her ears.

She coloured adorably as he repeated it again, and lowered her head when he murmured, almost to him-self, 'It's a delightful name. I hope that people do not shorten it to Kate?'

'Sometimes they do, yes.'

'You ought not to allow it.' His eyes strayed to the ring and he added, 'Is Dalton your family name?'

She frowned in puzzlement. 'Of course. What a strange thing to ask.'

The wailing rhythm of the *bouzouki* intruded into Kathryn's words and she wondered if he had heard them. If so, he made no remark on what she had said, offered no excuse for his question. Instead, he seemed to become absorbed in the music, his eyes moving from one mandolin-type instrument to another. The strains filled the room, mournful and sad, like a lament on the pathos of life. The floor show began, but very soon Kathryn decided she did not care for it and she turned to tell the Greek she was leaving.

It was as if he sensed her intention, because even as she opened her mouth, he was saying, 'Do you care for this, Kathryn?'

'No . . .' She stopped, becoming vexed by his familiarity. 'If you'll excuse me . . . ?'

'I'm leaving myself,' he said, rising at the same time as she. 'Let me buy you a drink.' It was a firm statement rather than a question, and again Kathryn's anger rose. What right had he, a total stranger, to speak to her like that?

'Thank you,' she returned coldly, 'but I'm going to my room straightaway. I've had a tiring day.'

She swept out, managing to find a pathway through the crowd watching the show. Her seat was pounced upon immediately, and so was the Greek's. He stayed beside her, though, close and proprietorial. He even took her arm when, turning as she left the room, she almost collided with a man carrying a tray.

'Steady, there,' he said. 'Come, let me buy you a drink.'

Her instinct was to throw him a sharp and acid retort, but instead she found herself saying, 'All right, then, but I'm not staying up late,' at which he gave a low laugh that brought the blood rushing to her cheeks.

'I don't intend to keep you up late, Kathryn,' he assured her in a tone that was now suave and, somehow, confident.

They drank at the bar, went from there to the dance floor, where they danced until midnight, and from there they strolled through the hotel gardens and stood beneath the star-spangled sky of Greece. The night was warm and balmy, the air filled with heady scents. It was a night for romance. . . .

Kathryn pulled herself up with a jerk. What had come over her tonight? She'd had no intention of spending hours and hours with the Greek . . . and yet it seemed quite natural that she should, just as it was natural for her to say, in answer to his low-toned question about meeting her the following day, 'Yes, I'd love to. Where shall we go?'

He made no answer but drew her to him, tilted her chin in an arrogantly masterful way that thrilled when it should have angered, and bent to press his lips to hers.

It was madness, she told herself half an hour later when, in her bedroom, she was staring at her face, her lips, her hair. She was flushed, and her lips were swollen and hurting. Her hair had been immaculate; it was more than a little tousled . . . and it was not as if she could blame the breeze for its condition.

As soon as she awoke the following morning, Kathryn's thoughts flew to the handsome Greek, and she felt excited at the prospect of seeing him again, looking forward eagerly to the excursion they were taking together. After showering, she dressed with care, choosing a skirt of lime-green cotton, crisp and new, with a matching sun-top. Her wide belt and sandals were white, as was her handbag. She used her blusher sparingly and only a touch of lip-rouge; her hair was given an extra brushing. Finally she used a perfume spray and, picking up her bag, went gaily to the lift, which took her down to the restaurant. Leon had said last night that he would see the headwaiter and have him arrange for them to share a table.

'It's much more pleasant if one has company,' he stated, and Kathryn found herself agreeing eagerly with what he said.

She saw him just as he spotted her. He rose from his chair, waiting until she was seated before he sat down again.

'Did you have a good night?' Leon asked with a smile.

'Yes, a very good night, thank you.' She smiled in response, aware of his appreciative eyes flickering over her . . . and finally coming to rest on the hand with which she was accepting the menu from the waiter at her side. It was the ring, she thought, wondering what his collection of jewellery was like. She loved antique jewellery herself, and could think of nothing nicer to collect if one was fortunate enough to be able to afford such an expensive hobby.

"Where are we going?' she asked him as they settled down to bacon, eggs and tomatoes, all done to a turn.

'Where would you like to go?'

'It doesn't matter. I haven't seen anything yet.' She paused to sip her coffee. 'Have you been to any of these sites before?' She was remembering that he had not told her what part of Greece he came from.

'I have, yes,' he answered, but added that he would enjoy seeing them again. 'Perhaps we'll go to Mycenae,' he went on. 'It's the highlight, after all.'

'Yes, indeed,' she responded eagerly. 'I've read so much about the fortress of Mycenae, with its royal tombs and all the beautiful treasures which the archaeologists found in them.'

'Most of the beautiful things you mention are now in the museum in Athens.'

He had his car, he had told her last night, and as soon as breakfast was over he took her to where it was parked, in the grounds of the hotel.

They got in and were soon bowling along the palm-lined avenue towards the gate leading out to the main road.

Leon drove through olive orchards and across wilder, arid country, all of it seeming to be very familiar to him. Kathryn, on the other hand, found every single aspect novel and exciting. Even a man and a heavily laden donkey brought an exclamation from her and several times she was conscious of her companion's swift glance of amusement as he drove along, smoothly covering the miles to their destination. They passed through Tiryns and Argos, travelling northwards through the Central Plateau of Peloponnesus, with mountain ranges towering all around.

'This is, of course, Arcadia,' Leon told Kathryn, smiling faintly. 'Where nymphs and shepherds danced to the merry pipes of Pan.'

'He was a nature god, wasn't he?'

'Yes; worshipped by the Arcadian shepherds because he made their sheep and goats fertile, and in addition caused the wild beasts to be killed.'

'It's fascinating—Greek mythology, I mean.'

Leon said nothing; he was negotiating a series of bends and his whole attention was on his driving. Kathryn, slanting him a glance, saw a rigid profile etched in lines both arrogant and noble. He was pleasant with her, a smiling companion of great charm . . . but, somehow, Kathryn had the firm impression that very different characteristics lay beneath the suave gentility which he was showing to her. In fact, she sensed latent pagan qualities that, if released, would dramatically transform his whole personality. Her thoughts switched to last night. He had taken her into the grounds of the hotel for one purpose. She had known he wanted to kiss her; and as she relived those vital moments before he had taken her in his arms, she found herself deciding that whatever this dark Greek wanted, he would get. . . .

He spoke at last, breaking into her thoughts as he began to tell her more about the god Pan—how he made his flute from reeds because the nymph Syrinx had escaped his attentions by being changed into a reed.

'He was more successful with the moon goddess, Selene,' went on Leon in his quiet, finely modulated accents. 'He dressed himself in the dazzling white fleece of a ewe and enticed her into the forest.' The amusement in his voice turned to laughter, and Kathryn laughed with him. She was thinking how pleasant this was—being with a handsome companion instead of wandering about on her own. For although she was happy when alone, she had to admit it was far more pleasant to have a man as charming and distinguished as Leonides Coletis as her escort. She was exceedingly flattered by his attention, marvelling that he should be bestowing it on anyone like her.

Eventually Leon turned off the main road into an avenue of eucalyptus trees which led to the village. Tobacco cultivation occupied all the lands in this region, and Kathryn became aware of Leon's repeated glances, from one side of the road to the other, as if the neat, widely spaced plants with their rigid stems and wrinkled leaves were of the greatest interest to him.

The village was reached, its aspect primitive in spite of a few recent buildings. Leon pointed out the celebrated hostelry—La Belle Hélène—in whose visitors' book could be found many famous names, including those of Virginia Woolf and, of course, the famous archaeologist Heinrich Schliemann. Because of his unshakable faith in the Homeric mythical tradition, Schliemann had excavated at Mycenae, and, having been successful in finding the most fabulous array of treasures, believed he had unearthed the tombs of King Agamemnon and his companions who had returned with him from the Trojan War. But Agamemnon had returned only to be foully murdered by his wife and her lover.

When the village was left behind, the citadel was

there before them. Perched on a hilltop above the Plain of Argolis, it was surrounded by a landscape of eerie bleakness, with the harsh mountain vistas of Zara and St. Elias creating a sort of primitive grandeur in keeping with the bloodthirsty history of the ancient fortress of Mycenae.

After Leon had pointed out the Treasury of Atreus, and the tombs of Clytemnestra and her lover, Aigisthos, he drove up to the front of the palace and parked his car.

Kathryn, looking around as she got out, thought she had never seen anything so austere as the aspect that confronted her—the grim isolation of the site, the harsh savage landscape of ravines and mountains . . . all combined to create a wild and eerie setting for a citadel whose blood-soaked history was known the world over.

The citadel looked forlorn and deserted, with no visible sign of its lost glories or the reason that it had once been called the 'palace of gold.'

'It's sad, isn't it,' Kathryn could not help saying, 'that the glory is all gone, lost in the mists of time?'

'Change, Kathryn,' responded Leon in emotionless, practical tones. 'Nothing survives the destructive encroachment of time, or its ravages.' He glanced around; Kathryn wondered if he found the aspect as bleak as she, if he felt the ominous atmosphere which the blood-ridden fortress still retained. His eyes were unmoving now, like a statue's. Tall and striking, he seemed like a god himself, for undoubtedly he possessed all the regal qualities of those awe-inspiring inhabitants of Olympus.

'All those terrible murders,' said Kathryn, shuddering as she glanced around, thinking of the foul slayings of Agamemnon and Cassandra and others who, arriving in their chariots from years of absence at the Trojan War, were joyously welcomed, then slain by his wife, the adulterous Queen Clytemnestra. 'How many murders took place here, Leon?' she asked.

'At least eight,' he said, and again Kathryn shuddered.

Leon turned and laughed. 'A great deal of blood has been spilled on the stones of this citadel.' He paused to regard her in some amusement. 'Shall I recite the list of murders to you?' he queried with a laugh.

'I expect they were pretty hideous crimes.' Kathryn glanced round the awesome place again, almost surprised to see nothing more frightening than a dog barking furiously at a group of tourists who had just arrived by coach from Corinth.

'You're quite right,' said Leon, 'they were pretty hideous. The worst, as everyone knows, was when, at the feast given by King Atreus for his brother, Atreus served him two of his own sons for dinner.'

'Oh!' Kathryn stopped and stared. 'You mean the brother's sons?'

'Yes, Thysetes' sons. It was said that the sky darkened that day, because of the appalling nature of the crime.'

Kathryn wrinkled her nose in perplexity. 'Was it real?' she asked uncertainly.

'Real?' They had begun to walk on again, to look over the fertile plain that swept down to the sea. 'What do you mean?'

'It's hard to separate fact from fiction.' Leon said

nothing, and she added, thinking of the slave girl Agamemnon had brought back with him from Troy, 'I felt sorry for Cassandra. She probably didn't want to come here at all.'

'Probably not, but she was part of the booty given to Agamemnon and so he brought her with him when he came home.'

'And she was brutally murdered by his wife.' At the sadness in Kathryn's voice, her companion looked down, regarding her with an odd expression as he said, 'Wouldn't you want to be avenged on your husband's mistress?'

'I'd never want to murder her,' answered Kathryn, but she frowned for all that and added, after a moment's thought, 'One never knows, does one, how one would feel in a situation like that?'

She was looking up into his dark face, and suddenly it was transformed, his features startlingly and frighteningly changed as a harshness spread over them, erasing the handsome good looks, the expression of amused tolerance which Kathryn had found so attractive on so many occasions, both last night and today.

'*I* certainly know how I'd feel!' he said, the harshness in his voice matching the expression on his face.

Startled by the dramatic change, Kathryn found herself saying in a faltering tone, 'You'd . . . want to kill your wife . . . if she was unfaithful?'

'Yes,' he replied without hesitation, 'I should want to kill her!'

'But of course you wouldn't kill her.'

Leon's eyes narrowed to mere slits as he said, 'By the

time I'd finished with her, she'd probably wish I *had* killed her.'

Kathryn shivered and walked on, unconsciously increasing her pace as if trying to get out of his way. But then she stopped to take in the view over the plain to the smooth dark sea of Greece. Leon was beside her again, and when she turned, all the harshness had left his face.

'Did I scare you?' he asked, those dark metallic eyes looking down into hers with a strange expression. 'I hope I didn't, Kathryn.'

'You certainly looked ferocious,' she said with a shaky little laugh. 'I wouldn't like to be your wife, Leon.'

'You'd have nothing to fear,' he rejoined, sounding casual enough now, and even indulgent, 'because you're not the girl to be unfaithful.'

She glanced at him swiftly, blushing at the compliment. 'No,' she said, 'I'm not.'

'You have a boyfriend?'

'Not anyone that I'm remotely serious about.'

'How old are you, Kathryn?'

'Twenty-two.'

'Young and beautiful.' He smiled, and she felt her pulses race. There was certainly something inordinately attractive about him, despite the change she had seen a few moments ago.

They wandered about the site for over two hours, with Leon explaining the layout in a way which convinced Kathryn he had been here not only once but several times. He told her of the golden doors that had hung on posts of gleaming silver, of the golden figures of youths holding flaming torches when banquets were held by the king. She wondered where all this gold had gone, and the sad thought occurred to her that it had long since been melted down for other—perhaps more practical—purposes. But if so many of these lovely things were gone, at least there was an enormous priceless collection of finds safely deposited in the museum.

Leon had been frowning slightly for the past few minutes, and presently he said, sweeping a hand to indicate another coachload of tourists coming onto the site, 'I was going to say we'd come back after lunch, but it's obviously going to be crowded this afternoon, and there's nothing that robs a site like this of its atmosphere more than crowds of people milling about with their cameras snapping incessantly.'

Kathryn nodded in agreement but said nothing. She would like to come back for another visit and decided to do so before the end of her holiday. 'I'll take you to the La Belle Hélène,' he said as they were strolling back to the car, asphodels and other wildflowers at their feet, growing in glorious profusion between the stones and at the sides of the paths.

The hostelry was crowded, but one of the proprietors instantly appeared, glancing at Kathryn for a second before greeting Leon like an old friend. Leon called him Demos and said he wanted a table for two if that were possible.

'In one moment there will be one for you—in a nice secluded corner of the garden!' the man promised, his dark eyes flickering again to Kathryn, this time to rove her figure, taking in the slender form, the youthful curves, the firm contours of her breasts. She coloured and glanced away, leaving the two men to chat in Greek for a few moments while waiting for the table that was coming vacant, its occupants already preparing to leave.

'Ah, now!' Demos led the way, and soon Kathryn and her companion were seated at the table where mulberry trees afforded them welcome shade from the grilling rays of the Grecian sun.

'It will be cleared and set in a moment,' promised Demos, speaking excellent English but with a more pronounced accent than Leon's. Another man came, and he too spoke familiarly to Leon. Kathryn wondered again where Leon lived.

'Do you come here often?' she could not help asking when the waiter had gone away with his loaded tray.

'Not often, but now and then.'

'It's lovely!' Kathryn was happy, and it showed all too clearly in her shining eyes, her delicately coloured cheeks, her rosy lips parted in a smile that was both spontaneous and youthful. Leon looked at her intently, an odd expression on his dark, handsome face. Did he find her attractive? she wondered, strange tremors rippling along her spine at the possibility.

'You're obviously enjoying yourself,' observed Leon, his eyes moving fleetingly to her ring. 'There's a lot more of this to come yet.'

A lot more. . . . This meant, surely, that he intended to spend the whole of the three weeks with her. He *must* find her attractive, then.

When coming on this holiday, she had expected to be

alone for the most part, at best finding a temporary companion, male or female, with whom to share the odd excursion, or perhaps a visit to the cinema. This companionship with Leon was something beyond her wildest dreams; she refused to think of the time, three weeks hence, when she would be saying good-bye to him. This was now, and she had no intention of dwelling on the void that the parting would inevitably leave.

Bouzouki music was being played by four musicians sitting on a raised wooden platform set to one side of the gardens; flowers abounded, colours flaring—the crimson of hibiscus, the pinks and whites of oleanders, the golden yellows of allamandas. From the tables came the multilingual babble of voices, with laughter often superimposed upon all other sounds. There was a carefree, almost festive air about the sunlit scene, and as she accepted the menu from the mahogany-skinned waiter, and her eyes met the admiration in her companion's expression, a wave of sheer undiluted happiness swept through her. She gave him a swift and winning smile which brought an instantaneous response. They gave their order. Leon had red mullet grilled over charcoal, and *souvlaki* flavoured with thyme. Kathryn had a Greek stew of beef and onions marinated in wine. It was called *stifado,* Leon told her. In addition, Leon ordered a variety of roasted meats and salads. Kathryn tasted such things as *dzadziki,* which was cucumbers soaked in yogurt, with dill and garlic; meatballs flavoured with nutmeg, olives and various cheeses and a rich Burgundy-type wine called Boutari.

Several lithe-limbed Greek youths came from somewhere behind the musicians and began to dance, twisting and diving and gyrating through the Zorba-style *syrtaki*. Then a couple more, linked by a handkerchief, their faces intensely solemn, rocked and dipped through the *tsamiko*, accompanied by the mournful strains of the *bouzouki* band.

Then one of the men lay down on the grass, abandoning his body to sexual movements. When he rose, there was a look of supreme ecstasy on his face, a sort of sublime joy and contentment. Leon, aware that Kathryn had been an unwilling spectator of this latest piece of activity, broke the silence that had descended upon them, telling her that all these dances were closely related to Dionysian rites as practised thousands of years ago.

'They're undoubtedly pagan,' he ended finally.

'Are all Greek dances pagan in origin?' Kathryn was grateful for his intervention.

'Most of them are a link with antiquity, yes. The dance was an integral part of their pagan religion, and, according to the expert on Greek dances, Dora Stratou, they have preserved their original movements in their entirety, all the archaic elements still intact.'

Kathryn, intensely interested, avidly wanted to hear more about the Greek dances. Leon told her about the dances of various regions of Greece, explaining how they differed from district to district.

'The dances of the Ionian islands are light and graceful, with swaying and gliding movements, while those of Epiros are more vigorous and heavy and are, therefore, rather slow. In Crete you see the war dance, the *pendozalis*, and until recently the dancers, all men of course, were armed. On the island of Cyprus the dancers often face one another, and here you have men dancing alone or women dancing alone. Not very often do men and women dance together.'

'It's strange to me,' she said, smiling. 'This separation of the sexes is very evident—with men everywhere and the women being conspicuous by their absence.'

He laughed with his eyes and Kathryn caught her breath. How devastatingly attractive he was when he laughed like that!

'The women are at home, cooking and mending and having babies,' he said. 'The men spend a great deal of their time in *tavernas,* playing *tavla* and drinking *ouzo.'*

Kathryn relapsed into silence, wondering what he did for a living. She found herself wondering about his home life, too, if he had brothers and sisters, a father and mother. She felt sure he had no wife, or even a girlfriend about whom he was serious. Other women friends . . . ? Well, she had heard about the Greeks and their pillow-friends, and she felt she would be very naïve indeed if she tried to convince herself that a man with the personality and obvious virility of Leon Coletis was living the celibate life.

The waiter was at their table again, removing the plates and all the side dishes, while another refilled their wineglasses, then handed them the menu so that they could choose their dessert.

Leon had the cheese board but Kathryn chose a fresh-fruit concoction composed of banana and pineapple slices and wedges of watermelon topped with cherries, cream and walnuts.

'That was delicious!' Kathryn leant back with a

contented sigh when she had finished, her eyes on the musicians, watching them individually—the man with the lute and the other with a clarinet. One man played a violin and the fourth a dulcimer-like instrument whose strings were struck by cotton-covered mallets.

'You're full, obviously,' commented Leon, who, Kathryn had noticed, had eaten sparingly.

'It was a lovely lunch. Thank you very much, Leon, for bringing me here.'

'A pleasure,' he returned, smiling. 'I little thought, this time yesterday, that I'd be here today, having lunch with a charming English girl. But there you are; one never knows what fate has in store for one.'

Kathryn coloured and lowered her lashes, shy all at once beneath his flattery. Was it genuine? Was she a gullible fool and he a wolf? She had heard a bit about Greek men, and how all they thought about was sex, which was why they stared so, with prolonged insolence, uncaring that you were staring back with contempt. Leon was not like that at all, although he did cast his eyes over her figure now and then, but with an appreciative glance, certainly not a sensual one. She was perfectly at her ease with him, thoroughly enjoying his company, feeling she had known him for weeks rather than hours.

At last they left the inn and sauntered over to the car park. The ground was rough, with small boulders strewn about, and Kathryn, although treading with care, managed to step upon one of these boulders and would have overbalanced if Leon hadn't seen what was happening and caught her before she fell. He brought her up against him; she felt the muscular hardness of his body, the strength of his arms, the cool clean breath that came from between lips that were touching her cheek.

'Oh . . . thank you!' she gasped, her heart pulsating at his nearness. 'I would have fallen . . .' She stopped and winced and glanced down at the ankle she had twisted.

'Did you hurt yourself?' asked Leon quickly.

'It's only my ankle. I wrenched it, I think, but it's nothing.'

'You'd better get into the car, and I'll take a look at it,' he said peremptorily. 'I hope you haven't sprained it.'

She hastily reassured him that no such injury had occurred, but limped painfully as they made their way over to where the car was parked beneath the shade of a clump of cypress trees. Leon told her to sit sideways on the seat so that he could examine the ankle.

'No, it's not sprained,' he pronounced after pressing and probing with his fingers. Kathryn, trying to retain an air of sophisticated calm, found instead that her pulses were hammering, her emotions wildly out of control. She looked down onto the top of his dark head as he bent over her foot, saw the broad, arrogant shoulders, dark-skinned beneath the thin white summer shirt he was wearing. He glanced up as he spoke, and his lips twitched because her cheeks were fused with delicate colour.

Perceptively, he knew she was deeply affected by the touch of his hands on her bare flesh. Slowly he straightened his lithe-limbed body to stand for a long moment regarding her with a strange expression in those darkly foreign eyes. Kathryn swallowed to get rid of the dryness affecting her throat. It was a tense and profoundly intimate situation even though he was not now touching her, and some thread of unconscious thought convinced Kathryn that Leon was as deeply affected as she. Did he like her? she asked herself again. Yes, she had already decided that much. Was it *more* than liking she saw written on his face at this moment . . . ?

Chapter Three

Another three days sped by on golden wings, with Leon and Kathryn spending every available moment together, taking sightseeing trips during the early part of the day when it was reasonably cool, then returning to Nauplia around three o'clock to spend the rest of the afternoon sunbathing on the beach and swimming in the clear blue sea. They dined at the hotel, then danced or watched the cabaret. Lastly they strolled in the cool, sweet-smelling garden, beneath an enormous moon and with the heady scents of flowers wafting about on the zephyr of a breeze coming down from a pine-scented hillside.

They kissed and embraced; Kathryn sensed a vigorously passionate nature beneath the strict control which Leon exercised over himself. They learned about one another—he that she was an orphan living in a flat, she that Leon owned a villa in Athens, that his business was tobacco and wine. He did not tell her at this stage that he owned all the tobacco-growing lands through which they had passed on their way to Mycenae, or the vinyards through which they had driven on another occasion. In fact, when she considered just how much he had told her about himself, she realised that it was very little indeed. But she herself had been fairly restrained as well, not going into any depth of detail about her life.

He was still exceedingly interested in the ring and had asked her again if she would sell it. She had refused.

'It's no use asking me,' she told him, firmly but with a hint of apology in her voice, 'because nothing would induce me to sell it.' She could have mentioned that she might one day give it away, to whoever had the rest of the set, but having voiced the lie that it had been in the family a long while, she naturally refrained from doing so. He had frowned rather darkly on her second refusal and a little access of dejection had fallen upon her as she realised that her refusal had actually angered him. She found herself recalling an earlier conviction that whatever this man wanted, he would get. Well, much as she liked him, Kathryn had not the slightest intention of wavering in her resolve not to part with the ring unless she found someone who had the other items in his possession. Not that she believed in the curse, but that had nothing to do with it anyway. This ring belonged with its fellows, and it would give Kathryn intense satisfaction if ever she did happen to come across the person who owned the rest of the jewellery.

Not that she cherished any real hope of doing so, but one never knew.

'I'd give you a very good price for it,' Leon had said, his manner persistent in spite of her firm refusal to part with the ring.

'I don't need the money,' she had assured him and watched his straight black brows lift as if he did not for one moment believe her.

'Everyone needs money,' he said reasonably. 'I'd give you far more than its market value.'

But Kathryn was shaking her head even before he had stopped speaking. 'Please don't keep asking me,' she begged. 'The ring is not for sale.' But she did wish she had not voiced that impulsive lie, for then it would have been possible to explain to him her reason for not wanting to part with the ring. However, she *had* voiced the lie, and there was nothing she could do about it.

More golden days passed. Leon took Kathryn to Tiryns, whose ancient past was reputed to be as distinguished as that of Mycenae. Legend had it that the city was built with the aid of the Cyclopes and, therefore, it must have been in existence before the founding of Mycenae. Kathryn, amazed by the thickness of the mighty walls, could very well imagine those giants having had a hand in the construction of the fortress.

'These walls,' Leon told her, 'were considered to be a wonder equal to the pyramids of Egypt.'

'They must have been incredible in their day!'

'The whole thing was incredible. There was a beautiful palace, with a vast courtyard behind it, and numerous buildings for the craftsmen necessary for the upkeep of such an enormous establishment. Come on,' he added, taking her hand in his, 'let us climb this staircase and look at the view from the top.'

Other trips included Argos and Corinth, and always there were the interludes spent on the beach, where, fanned by the cool breeze after the drive across the torrid plain, Kathryn invariably found herself lost in a world of sublime lassitude. There were other extremely pleasant afternoon interludes taken in a shady garden café where Kathryn and Leon would chat as they drank tea and ate sticky confections smothered in fresh whipped cream and nuts.

'Oh, but I shall remember this holiday for the rest of my life!' Kathryn made the exclamation one night when, after dining and dancing until after midnight, they emerged from the ballroom into the exotic atmosphere of the starlit gardens. 'I never thought it would be anything like this!'

Leon took her in his arms as soon as they were in their little secret place, and his hard lips possessed hers with the mastery that had thrilled her from the very first night.

'I'm glad you've enjoyed it as much as I have, Kathryn.' His voice vibrated with supressed ardour. During the time they had been together his manner had become more and more lover-like, and less and less restrained in the way he kissed and embraced her. His hard, muscular body had come to be familiar to her, and she accepted with a sort of joyful resignation the fact that he would hurt her, physically, by the passionate strength of his lovemaking. There had been moments of temptation, and one or two of real danger, for

Kathryn was no iceberg, although she had never even realised the height of her own ardour until she met Leon.

But he had been a gentleman throughout, much to her surprise, as in the very beginning there it had certainly occurred to her that she might find Leon wanting what she was unwilling to give. Had that turned out to be the case, it would without a doubt have been the end of the friendship.

One morning they explored the town of Nauplia, beginning with a stroll along the waterfront. It faced the land-locked gulf, and in the bay rose the Venetian castle of Bourdzi. Kathryn asked Leon if he knew anything about it and was told it was originally used as a fortress but, later, it became a home for retired executioners, a retreat for hangmen.

'But today it is a rather special kind of hotel,' he added finally.

Kathryn's eyes strayed again to the fortified islet. 'Why did the executioners want to live there?' she asked, puzzled.

'They didn't want to,' corrected Leon. 'But they weren't allowed to live in the town; the populace wouldn't have them.'

'Oh, they regarded them as . . . well . . . contaminated, did they?'

'I expect so. Whatever the reason—and I feel it might have had its roots in superstition—these men were made to live apart from their fellows.'

'And now it's an hotel. . . . I don't think I'd care to stay there,' decided Kathryn with a slight shudder which brought a twitch of amusement to her companion's lips.

'Ghosts can't harm you, child,' he said.

'No—for if they could, then no one would ever go up to the Acropolis of Mycenae,' she returned.

'Or most of the ancient sites of Greece.' They were leaving the harbour to wander towards the town itself, with its *cafeneions* and shops, its cinema that had once been a Turkish mosque, its Turkish fountain at the end of a steep alley.

'Can we look at the shops?' Kathryn put the question tentatively after they had strolled along in silence for a while, a companionable silence which was a new delight to her, since she had never experienced this 'oneness' with anyone before in the whole of her life. She seemed to be walking on air, resolutely refusing to admit that there was any time but the present. 'I know that men hate shops,' she added when Leon did not speak. 'And so if you—'

'I shall be delighted to look at the shops with you,' he interrupted. But he took her first to Constitution Square, where they sat beneath the shelter of the trees and drank chilled fresh orange juice. Most of the tables were occupied by locals, all men, smoking and drinking, playing *tavla* or fingering their worry beads, clicking them rhythmically from one end of the string to the other. Every eye was directed towards Kathryn as she and Leon walked through the medley of tables and chairs and people to take possession of a vacant table. Kathryn was by now used to these male stares, but at times wished she had brought a sack with her!

Time sped on relentlessly as one golden day followed upon another, and eventually Kathryn, living as she was in an ecstatic dream whose end she refused to contemplate, awoke one sunny morning to the knowledge that there were only three days left.

She showered and dressed in cool flowered linen—a sun-top above brief shorts, with an overskirt split to the waist at the left side. Her sandals were blue, to match the sprays of cornflowers running along the hem of the skirt; her bag was white, as was the Alice band she wore, which was more decorative than useful in keeping her long russet-brown hair in order. The breeze invariably played havoc with it, but Leon seemed to find the windblown effect more than a little attractive.

'You're not all joy today,' observed Leon later as, hand-in-hand, they wandered about the theatre of Epidauros after having driven the sixteen miles from Nauplia as soon as breakfast was over. 'What's wrong, my love?'

My love! Kathryn lifted her beautiful eyes to his, seeking, pleading, desiring. . . . She had no idea just when she had accepted the fact that she had fallen headlong in love with this handsome foreigner; all she did know was that, on waking this morning, she had admitted to a terrible fear, fear of the loneliness ahead, of a life into which no other man would ever enter. For her heart was lost, irretrievably, to a man she had known for only two and a half weeks. And now, as she caught and held his gaze, she was willing him to say the words she wanted to hear . . . words that would send her spirits soaring to the clouds.

She had no qualms, no cautious urge to probe deeper

into Leon's background. He was true and dependable, an honourable man. She knew it instinctively and she believed at this moment that nothing—absolutely nothing—could ever shake her faith in him. He had stopped, and, oblivious of any tourists who might be around at this fairly early hour, Leon bent to kiss her on the mouth. 'What is it, my little Kathryn?' he murmured as he drew away.

'I . . .' What was there to say in answer to his question? A man could say what was in his heart; he could ask her to marry him. But she was only a woman, and equality had not yet progressed to the point where a woman could make a proposal of marriage. Oh, she could, of course, but it would not be the *thing!* Leon would open his eyes in astonishment . . . and probably shy away, to escape while the going was good! So much for what the optimists of her sex called equality of the sexes, thought Kathryn, though not with any bitterness. She would not have proposed to Leon even if she had the right; she was old-fashioned enough to want to hear *him* propose and herself giving him her answer. But to look upon the situation realistically, she had no proof that Leon felt for her what she felt for him. This holiday, taken in the interesting and highly romantic atmosphere of ancient Greek culture, was the perfect setting for a flirtation . . . and Kathryn very much feared that Leon regarded what had passed between them as nothing deeper than that.

She had no one to blame for her foolishness in falling in love with him. He had never really tempted her; what she had given had been given freely, because she had *wanted* his kisses, his embraces, those endearing murmurs into her eager ears out there in the moonlit gardens of the hotel. They had found a secret little place among the trees, where pine needles provided a carpet, a fallen tree trunk a couch, and the argent moon all the light they needed.

'You haven't answered my question, Kathryn.' Leon's gentle voice drifted into her thoughts and she let fall a quivering sigh that caused his eyes to narrow perceptively.

'It's nothing,' she said at last. 'I suppose one always feels slightly depressed when a lovely holiday is nearing its end.'

'There are others to come. That's the way I always look at it.'

So casual, he sounded, and Kathryn's heart sank. Fool that she was, even to cherish one atom of hope that her feelings were reciprocated.

'You're right,' she returned, forcing a smile to her lips. 'There's always another time.'

'Shall you come to Greece again, Kathryn?'

'Of course. . . .' But she allowed her voice to trail away to silence, for she was not sure she *could* come again, not with these memories being so precious. No other visit would be the same. She thought that even were she to visit another part of the country altogether, she would be constantly reminded of Leon.

'You don't seem very sure.' He sent her a sidelong glance from under his dark brows. She sensed his knowledge of the way she felt about him, but there was nothing she could do about it.

'I'm not very sure,' she was honest enough to admit. 'You see, Leon, this has been so wonderful that . . . that . . . well, I m-might not . . .' Again her voice trailed away to nothing, the reason this time being the blockage in her throat. Her emotions were physically painful, and suddenly she wished she had never met Leon, had never experienced the wonder of this holiday . . . or the experience of love.

'I think,' said Leon, 'that I ought to take you to a café and get you a drink.'

She managed a smile then, and shook her head. 'I don't want a drink, thank you.'

'What do you want, Kathryn?'

'I don't know.' She lapsed into silence, and it was the voice of one of the guides that broke into her thoughts, and she found herself listening.

'The theatre here at Epidauros is the most perfect and best preserved in the whole of Greece. . . .' Kathryn heard no more, as Leon, holding her hand, was walking away. He disliked guides and tourists and always steered clear of them if it was at all possible. Nevertheless, they spent over three hours on the site, and Kathryn, trying to concentrate, heard Leon say that the cult here had been that of Asclepius, god of medicine, whose fame spread to Athens and other places, including the island of Cos. When at last they were coming away, Leon asked Kathryn if she had enjoyed it.

'Very much,' she answered truthfully. But she thought that now another day was more than half gone, and she could not help it if the tears gathered behind her eyes, could not be cold and philosophic about the holiday, telling herself that it was ridiculous for her to have supposed that something serious might come of it.

Thousands of couples met on holiday, enjoyed each other's company, then said good-bye at the end. She told herself again that she'd been foolish in the extreme. She ought to have guarded right at the start against falling in love with Leon.

But, she thought with a quivering sigh, love just comes, and you have no control, no armour with which to protect yourself against the dagger-points that pierce your heart.

In spite of Kathryn's adamant attitude over the ring, Leon had asked her twice more to sell it to him. As they left Epidauros, he asked her yet again, and this time there seemed to be an urgency about him that increased the puzzlement which had been growing upon her with his persistence. She had been so definite, so immovable, and yet he still tried to persuade her to let him have the ring.

'No,' she said determinedly when, having got into the car and pressed the starter, Leon turned to Kathryn and made another request that she sell him the ring. 'I can't think why you keep on asking me!' There was a trace of censure not unmixed with complaint in her voice, because each time this question arose, it caused a certain friction to enter into their relationship. 'You will never get it from me, so that's that!' It was the first time she had spoken sharply to him, and she could have wept as soon as the words were uttered. She saw his eyes harden, his lips become tight. He was angry—in fact, she had the impression that he was furiously angry, but he was managing to hide his anger, at least for the most part.

Nevertheless, his voice was curt and tinged with arrogance when he spoke. 'I should have thought, Kathryn, that you'd have sold it to me, if only as a gesture. It would remind me of this holiday—'

'You need reminding, then?' she could not help asking, the tears forming a cloud behind her eyes that hurt abominably.

'No, of course not, but it would be nice if I had the ring . . .' He stopped, brought to a halt because she had her head turned away.

Should she let him have it? She would never take any money for it, no matter what it was worth . . . but she could give it to him. . . . But no! Within seconds of that moment of indecision her resolve was as strong as ever. Why should she let him have the ring? He had enjoyed a flirtation with her; it was ended now, having meant nothing—*absolutely nothing*—to him, so was there any valid reason why she should give him the ring?

'No,' she said again, 'I shall never part with it!' Her wording was wrong. However, it didn't matter; all she wanted was to convince him, once and for all, that *he* would never get the ring from her.

Leon fell silent, and remained so all the way back to Nauplia. He drove into the grounds of the Hermes, but instead of telling Kathryn to collect her bathing suit while he went up for his trunks, he said stiffly, 'I don't feel like going to the beach today, Kathryn, I'll see you at dinner.'

Hurt by his coldness, and afraid she might show it, she sought refuge in pride. 'That's fine, Leon. I don't feel like going to the beach, either. I haven't had much opportunity for reading up till now, so I'll relax in my room with the book I brought with me.'

But once in her bedroom, the front she had put on collapsed and she shed a few tears of disappointment at not being with Leon this afternoon. It was the first time he had not eagerly sought her company, and she wondered if it really was because she wouldn't sell him the ring. It did not seem feasible that he'd react in this way, and after thinking about it for a while, Kathryn had almost convinced herself that Leon had got tired of her, in which case, she thought, he must be glad that her holiday was drawing to its close.

At dinner Leon was preoccupied but not unfriendly, and Kathryn hoped with all her heart that he had forgotten the slight unpleasantness of the afternoon, hoped too that he was now resigned to never owning the ring.

He talked to her amiably enough, but now and then he would lapse into brooding silence, drifting far away from her and from his surroundings, and frowning as if at some idea or thought which was far from pleasant. This was a new side to him; Kathryn wondered how many more facets of his personality she would see, were she to know him longer . . . and intimately. She did not think he had traits which she would find really unpleasant, although she was practical enough to admit that she could be wrong.

After dinner they danced as usual; then, to her surprise, Leon suggested they go outside. She had resigned herself to hearing him say that he was tired and wished to go to bed.

They sauntered to their secret place; he took her hand in the darkness and she thrilled to the strong grip as he curled his long fingers so that her small hand was fully enclosed within his. When they reached the hidden little arbour, he took her gently to him and kissed her on the lips.

But she sensed something different about him, something indefinable which filled her with a strange uneasiness. She wished the feeling were tangible, that she could put her finger on it, analyse it. His kiss was as thrilling as before, his embrace as possessive and masterful. And yet . . .

It was the same all the following day, and again on the last day of the holiday. Leon was as charming and friendly as ever, but Kathryn sensed some undercurrent, something savouring of a mystery, in his manner towards her.

On the final evening she dressed with her usual care, but her eyes had lost their glow, her lips their ready smile. Leon looked at her across the dinner-table, his gaze resting first upon her lovely curves, then on the beautiful arch of her throat against sloping shoulders whose only covering was that afforded by the cloak of silken hair. Her face attracted a longer perusal; she saw his eyes narrow and knew it was with perception. She was desperately unhappy, and it showed, just as her happiness had showed at the beginning of what was to be an idyllic holiday. All good things must come to an end. . . . What a sad quotation, she thought, quite unable to suppress the great shuddering sigh that rose from the very depths of her being.

She had accepted it, but her spirits were sunk so low

that she had the greatest difficulty in throwing off her dejection and adhering to her earlier resolve to make their final night together a memorable one.

Dinner was eaten in an atmosphere of strange tension, each endeavouring to contribute to the conversation, but they failed, with the result that there were inevitable lapses into silence. Looking at his dark, set face across the table, Kathryn felt convinced that he was equally as tense as she.

He held her close when, later, they danced; she felt his hand touch the ring she wore, knew he was very conscious of its presence on her finger. She thought of the lie she had told him and once again wished she could take it back so that she could explain why she must keep the ring just in case, by some strange trick of fate, she happened to come across the person to whom it really belonged.

'Let's go outside, Kathryn.' The words seemed to evolve from a decision suddenly reached, but it was the abrupt quality of Leon's voice that caught Kathryn's full attention. 'There are things I have to say to you.'

'To say?' Bewildering vibrations shot through her. 'Wh-what th-things, Leon?'

He held her from him, merely swaying to the rhythm of the dance music. 'Haven't you guessed, Kathryn?'

She shook her head, but it was an automatic gesture far removed from the more positive sensation that was swiftly taking possession of her, causing her heart to throb as the blood raced madly through her veins.

'Guessed . . . guessed what?' She swallowed, for her throat was dry, making speech difficult. Her eyes were scanning his face, searching for what she had dreamed of but never really expected to see.

'Come outside,' he repeated, bypassing her question. He was already steering her towards the open window, and within seconds they had left the sultry atmosphere of the crowded ballroom and were walking in the fresh cool air of a Grecian night.

Leon took her hand in his, curling his fingers, thrilling her with an unintentional show of his strength. The night was made for romance, for there was magic in the flower perfumes, in the towering mountains, softened by the purple radiance showered on them from a sky holding a million stars and the crescent moon hanging in their midst. Twinkling diamonds peeping through the trees proclaimed the presence of villas snuggling on the hillsides; from a rounded knoll rose a gleaming white church, its campanile clear and beautiful against the nebulous backcloth of the purple heavens as it swept on its natural arc to meet the dark horizon of the sea. The whirring of cicadas in the olive trees was an accompaniment for the mournful, persistent cry of a donkey tethered somewhere on a lonely hillside.

It was not until they reached their secret place that Leon took her in his arms and kissed her. 'Kathryn, you're so beautiful,' he murmured, his lips caressing her cheek. 'You know why I've brought you out here, don't you?'

She said nothing, and again she was brought close, her head tilted back so that he could possess her lips in a kiss that began in tenderness and ended in the sort of ruthless mastery that left her mouth bruised, and Kathryn gasping for breath. She turned in his arms, waiting for the words she so desperately wanted to hear. The breeze danced through her hair, teasing it into enchanting disorder; Leon slid his fingers through it in the most proprietorial way, savouring its silken softness before, gripping a handful close to her scalp, he tugged almost roughly, bringing back her head so that she was looking up into his face, helplessly unable to move without hurting herself. His mouth came down on hers, and within seconds his passion flared, ignited by Kathryn's own ardent desires as she pressed her slender body close to his. Leon's lips were tender one moment, merciless the next. Drawn into the vortex of a passion that was as pagan as it was irresistible, Kathryn thrilled to the dominance which left her in no doubt at all that Leon would always be the master, the one to be obeyed . . . or else. . . .

'Leon!' she managed breathlessly at last. 'You're . . . you're hurting me!' She glanced up; he hadn't expected her to, and she surprised a strange glitter in those grey, serpentine eyes, a brittle ruthlessness that sent an involuntary shiver running along her spine. Was he all he appeared to be? Fleetingly she allowed herself to be reminded of how little she knew this dark foreigner with the pagan background. But it *was* only fleetingly, since the thought was alien to the magic within her, the heady, exotic atmosphere of romance that surrounded her, her desperate desire to marry the dark aristocratic Greek who was holding her with such mastery, as if he were her husband already.

He said softly, his lips touching her ear, 'Will you marry me, Kathryn?'

At that she smiled up at him—a trusting smile, like that of a child who has not yet known the hurts of the world. And in her wide and limpid gaze there shone all the love she felt for him . . . the love and adoration.

'I'll marry you,' she returned, her voice husky with emotion. 'Oh, Leon, thank you for asking me!'

He said nothing, but again she surprised that peculiar glitter in his eyes. Her heart gave an uncomfortable lurch but she ignored it completely. Her head was in a whirl of excitement; clear thought was precluded anyway, because until a short while ago she had been suffering the agonies of despair, seeing only heartbreak as a reward of her foolishness in falling in love. She ought to know a lot more about the man she wanted to marry; she might be plunging headlong into something she would come bitterly to regret. . . . None of these thoughts had a place in the dream and the desire that was occupying her heart and mind and senses to the exclusion of all else. Leon affected her as no man ever had before or ever would again. She was his, come what may. Kathryn firmly believed that her destiny was irrevocably linked to his and she might just as well lose hold on life as lose this man whose magnetism drew her like a moth to a flame.

They talked for a while—in between Leon's passionate lovemaking—and Kathryn learned that Leon had only two relatives living, his mother and a sister, Marina, who, though only twenty-one years old, was an invalid. Kathryn also learned that the fields of tobacco through which they had passed on their way to Mycenae were his, as were the vineyards they had seen on another occasion.

He must be wealthy, decided Kathryn, wishing she could stay on for another few days so that she could see his villa in Athens, the house which would be *her* home before very long.

Kathryn told him more about herself, but somehow she had the rather baffling impression that he was not in the least interested in her background. Well, she thought, shrugging off her tinge of disappointment, it didn't really matter, for there was very little to tell anyway.

After a while she said, with a hint of shy hesitancy, 'When did you know you loved me, Leon? I ask because, only three days ago—when you said I wasn't all joy, remember?' He nodded and she continued, 'You didn't seem, at that time, as if you were thinking of asking me to marry you.'

'No, I admit it.' There was a rueful touch in his voice which Kathryn felt had been deliberately injected into it. 'You see, sweet, I was perfectly satisfied with my bachelor existence. It was so smooth and peaceful, and I hadn't any intention of allowing any woman to disrupt it. But you came into my life : . .' He broke off, and Kathryn saw a strange sort of frown crease his forehead. 'I had to have you, Kathryn, and so my bachelor days are at an end.'

She stared into his eyes, not knowing what she was searching for. 'Have you any regrets?' What had forced a question like that to her lips?

'None, obviously,' he answered briefly.

'Your sister, Leon—does she live with you?'

He nodded his head. 'We all live together, but if she wasn't an invalid, she'd have been married and Mother would have been able to remarry too.'

'Your mother has a . . . a friend?'

'She's had one for years, but she refuses to give Marina over to anyone else's care.' Bitterness edged his voice now, and the crease in his forehead was a deep furrow of reflective thought. Kathryn wished she could ask him to tell her what was in his mind, but she dared not.

'Will Marina never get better?' Deep compassion edged Kathryn's voice; she could not bear to think of a girl so young being an invalid.

A long unfathomable silence followed her question before Leon said, the oddest inflection in his voice, 'I don't know . . . time will tell. . . .'

'She's having treatment?'

'Treatment isn't possible, Kathryn, as the . . . disease . . . cannot be diagnosed.'

Kathryn looked at him, faintly puzzled by the hesitation. 'You mean,' she said, 'that the doctors don't know what's wrong with her?'

'That's exactly what I mean,' he replied, and there was something pointedly repressive in his voice that convinced Kathryn that he wanted the subject dropped. She thought she understood: any mention of his sister's illness would obviously upset him, so it was understandable that he preferred not to talk about it.

Chapter Four

The air was heavy with the scent of flowers and the sun was high in a brittle Grecian sky. As Kathryn stared into the distance, to where the Acropolis in all its glory flaunted the most beautiful building in the world, she felt as if heaven itself was hers.

The wedding had been quiet, with Leon's mother looking on with quiet and oddly unfathomable approval, and his sister in her wheelchair seeming to be happy for her brother even while a deep sadness darkened her eyes, and twice Kathryn had surprised a convulsive movement of her lips. Marina was beautiful —dark and sensitive features, gleaming black hair, expressive eyes which, her mother had told Kathryn, had at one time almost always been bright with laughter.

Kathryn had asked tentatively about the other girl's

illness; Mrs. Coletis had closed up immediately, and Kathryn, embarrassed, had never again broached the subject.

Leon was wonderful—the perfect husband and lover —and if at odd times Kathryn felt a twinge of uneasiness, she crushed it at once because she was sure there was no foundation for it.

'Darling . . .' Leon came to stand beside her on the balcony, his tall figure immaculately clothed in a lightweight suit of oyster grey, his shirt of snow-white cotton contrasting most attractively with the burnt-ochre of his skin.

Kathryn caught her breath and, as always, marvelled that she should have such a superlative man for her husband. How blessed she was!

'How about having lunch out?' Leon was close, his arm slipping about her waist in that gentle yet possessive way he always had with her. 'Mother's going out with her friend, and Marina wants to rest.'

'Your mother's going out with Demetrius?'

Her husband nodded. 'You like him, don't you?'

'Yes. He's charming.' Her mind wandered for a moment as she recalled how friendly the tall, greyhaired Greek had been with her from the very moment they met. He seemed . . . grateful in some way and yet expectant. Grateful. . . . Kathryn had pondered over this impression and found no explanation for it. 'I do wish he and your mother could marry.' Sincerity in her eyes and in her voice. Leon brought her to him and kissed her passionately on the lips while his hands caressed in the familiar gentle yet possessive way. From the beginning Kathryn had sensed that he would be wildly jealous if ever he thought she was interested in another man. She shuddered on recalling his attitude that day they were talking about Cassandra; Leon had openly admitted that he would want to kill his wife if she was unfaithful.

'Perhaps it will not be long before Mother and Demetrius can marry,' Leon said slowly, and at the cryptic note in his voice her eyes widened interrogatingly. But if Leon noticed the unspoken question, he chose to ignore it as he said, 'Well, are you ready for a trip to the Plaka?'

She laughed and put her hand in his. 'You know how much I love the Plaka. It's unique!'

'So much in my country is unique,' was his proud rejoinder.

They drove into the city and then Leon parked the car at an hotel from where they walked along to the Plaka. There was an exciting and yet mysterious quality about this ancient part of the great metropolis of Athens: the initial and strong impression that you were in the oldest quarter; the awareness of bustling life; the mob of hawkers crying out their wares; the flower-girls almost tormenting you with the thrust of their perfumed offerings against your nose; the doors agape and vendors beckoning you inside to buy 'antique' vases of bronze and copper authentically spattered with the evidence of age.

'We leave them in the river for up to two years,' one very honest shopkeeper told Kathryn when she said defiantly that he was trying to pull a trick on her.

Leon bought a sprig of jasmine and stopped to pin it onto his wife's dress. It was an intimate moment, with his face above hers, and her eyes, limpid and filled with love, staring into his. Ignoring the crowds around them, he bent his head and kissed her softly parted lips.

The restaurant to which they went was the Donoussa, where they lunched on the flower-bedecked roof and looked over the vast complexity of the city. Leon ordered *moussaka,* which they ate with a beetroot salad, and they drank fruity Greek wine to wash it down. The dessert was a salad of watermelon, bananas and pineapple slices canopied with lashings of cream, walnuts and cherries. There were six musicians on the dais—two *bouzouki* players, two violinists and two with tambourines. In the dancing space, four men performed, with their leader twisting and rocking, ecstasy on his face as if he actually experienced the erotic pleasure depicted by the sexual heaving of his groin as he rotated it with the sheer abandonment of those ancient pagans who had first performed the dance according to Dionysian rites. He was perspiring profusely when at last, to a spate of applause, he went off after bowing several times, a sort of rapturous joy on his Arab-brown face.

Kathryn, used by now to the erotic nature of most Greek dances, felt her colour rise all the same.

Her husband smiled in some amusement and said, 'How delightfully innocent you are.'

'Not innocent,' she denied, 'but a trifle embarrassed.'

'Or just shy?' His eyes fell to the ring she wore above her wedding ring. He had said he would buy her an engagement ring, but for some reason she had wanted to wear the one she had found.

However, when they were strolling back to where the

car was parked, Leon stopped at a jeweller's and said quietly, 'I've had a word with Kostos Stomati about a ring for you—'

'A ring? Oh, but—'

'Darling,' he interrupted softly but in firm accents for all that, 'it is my wish that you have an engagement ring. Come, my love. . . .' He took her arm and she was ushered into the shop.

Kostos came forward and smiled the familiar golden smile.

'I have brought my wife, Kostos, and we want to choose something very special,' Leon said.

'Of course.' Kostos' eyes rested on the diamond-and-sapphire ring and he whistled softly. 'Oh, but this is beautiful and . . . and what you say . . . uncommon, no?'

'Unusual,' supplied Kathryn. 'It's very old.'

'But you want another?'

'Kathryn needs an engagement ring,' from Leon almost curtly. There was a strange glint in his eyes and his mouth was tight. It was plain that he was not pleased that Kostos should be so interested in Kathryn's ring. He turned to her. 'I never asked your preference. Do you want another ring with sapphires and diamonds—or something different?'

She wanted only to wear the one she had found, but naturally she refrained from saying so. Leon wanted her to wear his ring, which was only natural, she thought understandingly. But her smile was forced and an unwanted heaviness lay upon her, detracting from the enthusiasm she should have been feeling at a time like this, when she was to choose her engagement ring.

She could not have chosen sapphires, so she said she would like a ring of diamonds and rubies. A tray was brought and it was then that Kathryn came to realise that she would not always be feeling like this—apathetic and faintly resentful. One day she would treasure her engagement ring and, therefore, she applied herself to making the kind of choice she would not regret.

'This one. . . .' It was a heart-shaped ruby surrounded by diamonds. 'It's too large, though.'

She was twisting it on her finger, and Leon said, nodding as he agreed fully with her choice, 'That's no problem.'

'None at all,' from Kostos. 'It will be ready in one or two weeks.'

'You're quite happy with it?' Leon asked the question as they were driving back to the villa in the car.

'Yes, of course.' She wanted to thank him, but somehow the words would not come. Her throat was tight and it burned. She wanted to cry and chided herself for the way she was feeling.

Silence enfolded them after that as they became absorbed by their own private thoughts. Kathryn's mind went briefly to the charming flat she had left, to the incredulity of her friend Carole when she had related all that had happened on the holiday.

'And now you're getting married!' Carole had exclaimed, shaking her head. 'I can hardly believe it!'

Nor can I, Kathryn had thought, wondering if she would wake to discover it had all been a dream.

'You haven't known him long,' Carole had murmured later, doubt edging her voice. 'Marriage is so risky, Kathryn.'

Kathryn had laughed lightly, and her voice was confident when she replied. 'For others, yes, but not for me. Leon's a wonderful person and I love him with all my heart.'

Carole had shrugged and wisely said nothing. Kathryn had had the impression that she would have liked to proffer advice but knew it would fall on deaf ears.

'You're very quiet.' Her husband's voice recalled her from the past, and Kathryn turned to look at him.

'I was thinking about Carole and her surprise when I told her I was getting married.'

'Your friend from the flat below,' he said, but without much interest. His eyes had rested momentarily on her hand, which was flat on her knee. The ring again. She said, voicing something she had wanted to say for the past two weeks, ever since her wedding day, 'Your collection of jewellery, Leon—I'd love to see it.'

He seemed to stiffen, but the impression was soon dismissed. 'Of course, dear. At present it's in the bank, but one day I'll get it out so that you can see it.'

'In the bank?' with some surprise. 'But you have a huge safe at home. Marina was telling me that all her jewellery is in there.'

'So it is.' Leon became fully absorbed in his driving for a few silent moments; and then, 'Talking of Marina —it's her birthday in a couple of weeks' time.'

'It is? Oh, then I must buy her something.'

Another silence, strange and disturbing in some indefinable way. 'She was saying just how much she admired your ring.' Slow the words, and soft. Kathryn felt a quiver pass along her spine.

'You're suggesting I give it to her?' she said repressively. 'I have said many times that I cannot part with it, Leon.'

'You'd not really be parting with it. I mean, it would still be in the family.'

She leant back in her seat, her expression thoughtful. 'I am not giving my ring to anyone!' she said at last, anger bringing colour to her cheeks. 'First you wanted it for yourself, and now you want me to give it to your sister! I'm keeping it, so please do not mention it ever again!' She was almost in tears, regretting her anger and sharp words and yet at the same time feeling she had been forced to utter them.

'I see,' with an icy inflection.

'Then it's more than I do. There's some mystery about your obsession to obtain this ring.' She paused, and then, curiosity mingling with her anger, said, 'Is that why you wanted me to have an engagement ring?'

'Certainly not! It's a natural thing for a man to buy his fiancée a ring. You decided you didn't want one and I let you have your own way, but now I have changed my mind. I want you to wear *my* ring.' Cold the tone, and imperious. It was very plain that her attitude infuriated him. Was there some mystery? she asked herself. If so, what could it be? She shook her head, dismissing the idea as fanciful.

That evening at dinner Leon was silent for most of the time, but Marina was rather more talkative than usual, and so was her mother.

'Did you have a nice time this afternoon?' Mrs. Coletis inquired in her deeply accented voice.

'Yes, it was lovely. We had lunch in the Plaka.'

'I used to spend hours in the Plaka,' reflected Marina. 'It has a sort of mystic attraction and yet there's a self-evidence about everything—the shops and their vociferous owners; the clever guys who are out to con you; the flower sellers who won't take no for an answer; the slow-walking priests of the Orthodox Church whose beady eyes are stripping you—'

'Darling!' gasped her mother, horrified. 'That is enough!'

'All Greek men strip you,' continued Marina undaunted. 'I was in England once and the men there treat their women with respect.'

'It's probably all a pose, dear.'

'Not at all. I would like to marry an Englishman . . .' Marina stopped suddenly, and several puzzling things caught Kathryn's attention. First was the abrupt halt of Marina's sentence, just as if for a moment prior to it she had been carried away totally by the probability of getting married despite the fact that she was ill; second, there was the almost startled glance her mother gave her, a glance which was transferred to Leon. His eyes had fixed themselves on Kathryn's left hand, where the ring glittered in flawless beauty in the light from the candles on the table.

Silence fell, became intense—electric almost—then was sharply broken by Leon's voice, which was accompanied by the clapping of his hands to call Davos, the manservant who was serving them their dinner. 'Pour the wine,' he ordered curtly, and then shifted his gaze, deliberately avoiding his wife's bewildered eyes.

She glanced around, saw that Marina was busy cutting her meat, while her mother was absently crumbling a bread roll. Nerves quivered along Kathryn's spine, and she frowned heavily because she could not explain anything—why she was feeling tense like this, why the other women seemed uncomfortable, why Leon's forehead was creased in a frown.

Much later Kathryn questioned him, but he simply looked askance at her, and she knew he was in no mood for giving explanations.

The following morning Kathryn said to her sister-in-law, 'Marina, I was puzzled last evening when you spoke of the possibility of your getting married. Has there been some improvement in your condition lately?'

It was a long time before the Greek girl spoke, for she seemed to be considering carefully, as if trying to make a decision. But then she merely said quietly, 'No, not anything . . . er . . . noticeable, Kathryn.'

Kathryn's eyes narrowed slightly as she examined the other girl's expression. That she had lied was certain . . . but why? 'Leon said you have a birthday coming up soon,' said Kathryn, deciding to change the subject. 'Is there anything special you would like—or do you prefer a surprise?' Strangely, until this moment Kathryn had forgotten all about Leon's telling her that his sister would like to have the ring, but now it flashed back into her memory as Marina's eyes went instantly to her finger.

'That ring. . . . It's awful to ask for something someone else owns and treasures, Kathryn, but . . . but I would love to own it. . . .' She shook her head, and a heavy frown creased her brow. 'No . . . no, I must not ask such a favour!'

It was Kathryn's turn to frown as she said slowly, 'Why do you want it so much?' she inquired, her eyes focused on the other girl's face because she had no intention of missing one change, one flicker of an eyelid. 'Your brother wanted it very badly and asked me several times to sell it to him. And now you want it. What I want is to know why both you and Leon are so anxious to get it from me.'

There was another long pause before Marina spoke, and when she did eventually break the silence, there was a solemn note of resignation and despair in her voice. 'It is just that I like your ring, Kathryn, and would love to own it. But I can understand that you do not want to part with it, and I should not have asked. As for my birthday—well, I think I would like a surprise.' A lovely smile spread over her face, but Kathryn was frowning heavily as, ignoring this last sentence, she persisted.

'Your brother badly wanted to buy this ring from me, and it's plain that there is some important reason why both he and you have this desire to get it from me.'

Marina moved awkwardly, and painfully, judging by the sudden tightening of her lips, in her chair, but there was nothing to denote pain in her accents as she said, adopting an attitude of lightness designed to deceive but which quite naturally failed because by now Kathryn was wholly intrigued by this interest in her ring, 'I expect Leon, knowing my taste in jewellery, thought he would buy your ring to give me pleasure . . .' She broke off and smiled as she shrugged her shoulders. 'It isn't important, Kathryn. Let us talk of something else.'

'Leon said he wanted the ring to add to a collection of antique jewellery he had,' supplied Kathryn, again ignoring Marina's last sentence. 'He never mentioned anything about pleasing his sister.' Her voice had taken on a hard, determined edge, but Marina seemed not to notice, for her eyes had become vacant and a deep sigh left her lips. 'I want to know more about this desire to have my ring, Marina.'

The other girl, looking up from her chair, gave another sigh and shook her head. Kathryn's attention was keenly arrested by the dark, intense face, the resignation settled in eyes that were anxious, too. It was very plain that Marina regretted the mention of the ring.

'Please, Kathryn,' she pleaded as Kathryn's manner remained coldly deliberate and determined. 'Please let the matter drop.' And with that Marina began to wheel herself away towards the open window of the lovely salon where they had been talking. Kathryn's eyes narrowed as she watched her, moving quietly in the chair. Undoubtedly there was some mystery. But it was only two days later, when she overheard a conversation between Marina and her mother, that Kathryn wondered why she had been so stupid as not to have guessed the reason that Leon wanted the ring. But how was she to have known that he had the rest—or rather that Marina had the rest—of the jewellery? This was

Greece, and the jewellery had been made in England for a family who lived there. . . .

Kathryn was strolling in the gardens of the villa when, from behind a thick, high yew hedge, she heard voices. She would have proceeded, but on hearing her name, she naturally slowed her steps and then halted abruptly, the fine gold hairs on her arms rising as if in sympathy with the increasing rate of her heart beat.

' . . . Leon was very wrong to marry Kathryn in order to get the ring, Mother. She is too nice to be treated like that.'

'But, dearest, he was thinking only of you.'

'And not worrying that he was marrying Kathryn without loving her. She's English, Mother, and English girls want love in their marriages. Kathryn loves my brother dearly, and it makes me cry to know that he does not love her.'

'He treats her well, dear—'

'But loves another!' broke in Marina fiercely. 'He loves Eugenia; you know that!'

'His affair with Eugenia is finished, my dear.'

'Is it?'

There was a pause, and Kathryn, her legs like jelly and a searing pain spreading through her head, moved slowly towards a little rustic seat and sank down into it.

'Christos told me that they met when Leon went to Glifadha the other day. He saw them together—'

'You have been talking to Christos?'

The older woman's voice had sharpened, but that of her daughter was calm as she said, 'He telephoned me,

Mother. You would not have me give him up when he still loves me?'

'You know very well he has someone else. Marina, dearest, you only hurt yourself by clinging to the hope that one day you and Christos will marry. He is half-English, remember, and one day might decide to leave Greece and settle in his mother's country.'

Kathryn felt she had heard enough, and yet she could not rise, for not only was her body weak, but her mind too was in a state of torpor. She found it impossible to think at all, much less think clearly. But at least this place where she was sitting was peaceful, with birds twittering in the trees and cicadas murmuring in the distant olives which formed a copse close to the orchard where the citrus fruits grew—the juicy oranges and shiny green lemons. If only these two would move on. . . . But they were speaking again, and Kathryn learned that Marina's illness had come about only after she had been told of the curse by an antique dealer she had met when she was on a visit to London. She had been wearing the necklace and earrings at a party she had been invited to. The man had come to her, asking about the jewellery. Marina had said that her father had bought it from Christie's several years ago, and it was then that the antique dealer revealed the story of the curse. From that day Marina had brooded, then after a month or so had turned in on herself. Another month, and she said she felt ill, and then her legs became weak. After a while she took to the chair. Doctors were baffled; they could do nothing for her.

All this Kathryn heard as the two talked on the other side of the hedge. And then they moved; Kathryn could imagine the mother propelling her daughter's chair instead of allowing Marina to do it herself.

Reaction set in as soon as she knew the two were away from where she sat, anger and pain battling for supremacy. Kathryn's heart was aching because of the revelation that Leon had merely used her, married her in order to get the ring, to complete the set and so exorcise the curse. But it puzzled her that he could be affected by superstition, for he seemed to be a totally rational person, practical and contemptuous of such things as curses. Somehow it did not make sense. And yet, there was no denying he had married her to obtain the ring.

He did not love her and, looking back, she saw so many instances of doubt, when she had told herself that the holiday was to him nothing more than a flirtation. Well, she knew now that his initial interest had stemmed from his catching sight of the ring. When he joined her to watch the cabaret, he had then examined the ring and knew for sure that a miracle had occurred: he had found the person owning the missing item of jewellery. If she had sold or given him the ring, that would have been the end as far as Leon was concerned . . . and he would have been free to go to the woman he was in love with. He had sacrificed his own happiness and hers in order to make his sister well. Again Kathryn was in doubt that Leon could be so superstitious, and yet he must be, for otherwise he would never have gone to the lengths of contracting a loveless marriage.

Loveless? Kathryn's mouth curved bitterly and her anger increased. For the knowledge that her husband knew that she loved him was almost unbearable. How he must have laughed at her naïveté! A stupid, starry-eyed girl falling head over heels in love with a man she had met casually while on holiday. The more she thought about it, the more her anger grew, until at last she could wait no longer to confront him and tell him what she thought about him—his contemptuous behaviour, his heartlessness in pretending he loved her just so she would marry him.

She searched for him in the house, but as he was not about, she concluded he was in his study. What must she do in the light of the knowledge that had come to her? she asked herself as she made her way along a wide corridor to the room at the very end, the room with one of the best views in the house. She would leave him. . . . Yet why should she? Where would she go and how was she to find a post even half as well-paying as the one she had given up?

She had not yet come to any conclusion when she knocked on his study door.

'Come in.'

She pushed the door inward, then stood in the threshold for a while, looking at him sitting there at his big antique desk, his face a study of arrogant superiority, his eyes coldly inquiring—or so it seemed to Kathryn's imagination.

'I know you hate being disturbed—'

'I am rather busy, Kathryn.'

Her chin lifted at that, and a sparkle leapt to her eyes. She walked into the room and stood by the desk. 'What I have to say is important. I intend to say it whether you are busy or not!'

He stared uncomprehendingly. 'Is something the matter, dear?'

'Dear!' She cast him a scornful glance. 'You can cut out the pretence, Leon,' she said. 'It must have been an irksome strain to pretend you loved me!'

He stood up, crimson threads creeping up along the sides of his mouth. 'Just what is this?' he demanded, and the arrogant tone only added fuel to the fire of his wife's anger.

'I happened to overhear a conversation between your mother and Marina. Marina had already asked me to give her my ring as a birthday present. I know now why you married me . . .' She broke off and laughed, loudly and hysterically, her nerves out of control. 'It's a joke, really! Oh, such a joke on you! Because, you see, the only reason I would not part with the ring was that I hoped one day to find the owner of the rest of the set of jewellery!' She laughed again, and now Leon came swiftly to her side of the desk. She sidestepped him on realising he was about to adopt the usual method of curing hysterics. 'Just you dare lay a finger on me and I shall scream the house down,' she threatened.

He stopped, lowering his hand. 'You say you overheard a conversation between my mother and sister? You mean, you deliberately eavesdropped?'

'You can also cut out the contempt! Yes, I did eavesdrop, and I have no regrets! I learned all about the beginning of Marina's illness after she had heard of the curse. It's very puzzling to me, though, that you yourself can be so superstitious. Why, the curse is nothing but rubbish!' She was reminded of the professor's words, his attitude towards the curse, and towards those students who had ridiculed it. Was there really something in it? Kathryn found herself beginning to have doubts and fears, and a shiver passed through her. She had always shied away from things like the occult, or ghosts or anything that savoured of the supernatural. She had always tried to ignore the prophecies of Nixon, but now . . .Well, so many of that mad young man's predictions had come to pass . . . and surely it could not be mere coincidence.

'I am not superstitious.' His voice was low and controlled, but the glitter in his dark eyes plainly revealed the anger within. 'But my sister is, and when I saw the ring on your finger, I felt I must have it—'

'As I've said, you need only have mentioned that you had the rest of the set and you could have had it.'

She stared into his face, noticing the tautness of the features which made the smooth olive skin seem so tight that there might not have been any flesh at all over the high, prominent cheekbones.

'So that's why you were so adamant. . . .' He spoke to himself, and it did appear to Kathryn that deep regret echoed in his voice.

'What a waste,' she cried, anger and pain adding a high-pitched note to her accents. 'You gave up the woman you loved and married me when there was no need! But now you're tied, Leon—and you will remain tied because I shall never leave you!' Her wild, uncontrolled fury was leading her to say the first things that entered her mind. She wanted to hurt, as she was being hurt; she wanted to convince him that he would never be free, that he would live out his entire life in regret. 'How you must be gnashing your teeth! You duped me, but you'll pay for it—and you'll continue to pay for the rest of your life!' She tugged at the ring, took it from her finger and threw it across the desk, watching as it slid away and dropped to the floor. 'Take it! Give it to your sister—and I hope she enjoys wearing it—'

'Shut up!' Leon spoke at last, and it was as though he felt she was hurting herself just as much as she was hurting him—or trying to hurt him. 'There's much you do not understand, Kathryn. Oh, I realise that at this moment you feel you know it all, because it appears simple, but you know very little.' He looked steadfastly at her, his anger dissolved. 'I want you to believe that there are certain aspects which you are in the dark about.'

He paused, and after a silent moment she asked, pain thickening her voice, pain that seared her heart and rose to block her throat, 'You married me for the ring? You had no love whatsoever for me?'

It was a few seconds before he replied, 'I did marry you for the ring.'

'Married me without love?'

'I did not love you, no,' he admitted frankly.

She closed her eyes as pain shot through her body. Only now did she realise, with a sense of shock, that, deep within her she had cherished the hope that even though Leon had wanted the ring he had loved her a little as well. But now he had baldly admitted that love had never entered into it; he had married her for his sister's sake.

'You lied when you said you collected antique jewellery.' She had no idea why she should suddenly have recollected a thing like that, for it was of minor importance beside the momentous happenings of the past hour or so.

'I couldn't think of anything else at the time,' he admitted. He seemed to be tense, but in no way unsure of himself, and this Kathryn resented. She felt he should be repentant, humble, in fact. But he portrayed neither emotion. On the contrary, it seemed to Kathryn's unhappy mind that he was as arrogant as ever, that he cared little for the way she had been hurt.

'Your sister's illness has nothing to do with the curse,' she began, but her husband interrupted her.

'Unfortunately, it has. I firmly believe it's a psychological phenomenon, but there is no doubt at all that Marina's illness was brought on because she had heard of the curse. The doctors are baffled and so have given up trying to do anything for her. But it's my firm opinion that once she has the ring, she will begin to throw off this malady which has well nigh ruined her life and that of my mother.' So serious the tone and the look in his eyes that for a space Kathryn forgot everything except the pressing matter of her sister-in-law's illness.

'She actually believes in the curse?'

'You know she does. You heard enough—or so it appears to me.'

She nodded thoughtfully. 'My professor believed in the curse—well, perhaps not exactly, but he did not ridicule it.'

'Professor?' with interest and an interrogating glance. 'What are you talking about?'

'I forgot . . . you don't know how I came by the ring.' She went on to tell him everything, watching his changing expression, his surprise which turned to astonishment when she related what happened on her visit to the home of the St. Cleres in Lincolnshire.

'So *he* obviously believed in the curse,' he said when at last Kathryn had finished speaking.

'Not only believed, but was afraid of it. He couldn't get me out of the house quickly enough.'

Leon looked curiously at her. 'You yourself were never afraid?'

'Of course not,' she answered derisively. 'I enjoyed wearing it. . . .'

She allowed her voice to trail away to silence, and Leon said sharply, "Are you sure you weren't afraid?'

'Not—not at the time. I mean . . . no, I haven't ever been afraid because I felt that the curse could not affect me, but now . . .'

'Yes?'

'I don't know. . . .' She spoke slowly, every nerve in her body tingling. "If . . . if it hadn't b-been for the ring, then . . . then you'd not have married me and . . . and I'd not be in th-this mess.' All the fight and anger had gone out of her because she was now totally absorbed by the ring, and the curse attached to it. 'It looks very much as if . . . as if the curse really is effective.' She looked at him, her face pallid, her eyes dull and scared. 'This marriage . . .'

'You're not in a mess, as you term it,' Leon assured her. 'You are married to me, and this is your home; you're secure for life—'

'Yes, but if this has happened, then what might happen next?' There was a wild and frantic quality about her that brought her husband close, and he reached out to take her hand in his, reassuringly.

His foreign voice was gentle and soothing as he said, 'The jewellery is all together, Kathryn, so you have nothing to fear.'

'I don't know . . . Oh, it is all stupid! No matter what the professor or that stupid Sir Algernon thought! There are no such things as curses!'

'I firmly agree.'

'Then why did you trouble to get the ring into your family?'

'Because, Kathryn,' he answered with some asperity, 'my sister *does* believe in curses—at least the curse attached to this jewellery. It was from the moment she heard of it that she became a different person—nothing too noticeable for a week or so, but gradually she became morose, quiet, and would scarcely speak when spoken to. Unknown to either Mother or me, she managed to contact this antique dealer again after she left England, and he wrote to her all about the misfortunes which had befallen the various owners of the jewellery. Marina became ill—really ill, Kathryn; there was no doubt about it, and she became worse as the weeks and months went by, until she actually lost the use of her legs.' He paused a moment, but Kathryn was too intrigued to interrupt, and he continued. 'It might seem incredible to you, as it would to me if I had not seen it for myself. I've just said I firmly believe it's pyschological and brought on entirely by Marina herself, and there have been times,' he went on with grim, reflective stress, 'when I could have beaten her, tried to knock some sense into her, but it wouldn't have been any use.'

Kathryn said, 'It's rather like those natives who die when someone sticks pins into their effigies, or hangs them.'

To her surprise, a smile touched the chiselled outline of her husband's mouth. 'Not quite the same, but you have a valid point of similarity. However, we shall see what happens now that Marina has the ring.' He paused, and they both glanced to where it lay on the carpet by the corner of the desk. 'It would be better if you gave it to her,' he suggested, and Kathryn nodded and moved to pick it up. She straightened and was close to her husband. Tears formed a cloud at the backs of her eyes, but it was accusation that looked out from their depths and which rendered her voice husky.

'What about us? I'm not willing to be a proper wife to you anymore.' She was brave to say a thing like that, she knew, but the very thought of sleeping with Leon now that she knew he had no love for her was repugnant, to say the least.

'What exactly am I to infer from that, Kathryn?' he inquired with cool deliberation.

'I can't sleep with you, knowing you don't love me.'

He frowned and sighed, and for a long moment regarded her in silence. 'We've been happy enough so far,' he pointed out. 'I don't see why we shouldn't continue as we have been doing.'

Her chin lifted and sparks lit her eyes. 'You seem to forget that I believed you loved me.'

He turned away, and she could not resist broaching

the subject of the girl he had let down when he had decided to marry in order to get the ring.

He swung around and glowered at her. 'How the devil do you know about Eugenia?' he demanded, forgetting that she had briefly mentioned the girl already.

'That was something else I overheard. Marina stated quite emphatically that you loved her.' A small moment of indecision, and then Kathryn added, watching his face closely, 'You were with her in Glifadha—someone called Christos saw you together.'

His mouth went tight. 'There is no longer anything between Eugenia and me,' he said firmly. 'The meeting was a chance one. I had no idea Christos saw me with her.'

'I can't believe you have given her up completely.'

'Kathryn, I happen to be married to you!'

'Christos,' she murmured, feeling it were better to veer the subject. 'He's a friend of Marina's it would seem?'

'He's in love with her, and if it hadn't been for this illness, she'd have married him. I believe I mentioned something about it to you before?'

She nodded reflectively. 'Your mother said he has now found someone else, so how can he be in love with Marina?'

'He has a pillow-friend. One cannot expect him to live the life of a saint simply because Marina's so stupid as to allow herself to become ill as she has.' Short the tone, and impatient. It was clear that, although he had a certain sympathy for his sister, he had little or no patience with the superstitions which had been responsible for her having taken to a wheelchair.

'I don't admire him for having a pillow-friend!'

'He'd not expect you to,' was Leon's smooth rejoinder. 'What you think wouldn't interest Christos in the least.'

She coloured to the roots of her hair as the snub went right home. She glared at Leon and reiterated her intention of not sleeping with him anymore. 'It would be immoral,' she added, knowing that would annoy him.

'Immoral?' with a fractional lift of his straight black brows. 'You're my wife. And if I decide to assert my rights, then I shall do just that.'

She coloured again and turned from him. 'I'll leave you to your work,' she said stiffly. 'I'm going out.'

'Out? Where to?'

'I don't know. I want to think.'

'Well, don't stay out too long. Marina's come to depend on you for company.' His eyes dropped to the ring she held in her fingers. 'Are you going to give her that?'

'Yes—for her birthday.'

He waited a few seconds before saying, quietly and with an edge of gratitude to his voice, 'Thank you, Kathryn. Let us both hope and pray that what's happened hasn't been for nothing.'

She looked at him across the space separating them, her lips moving convulsively. 'I've been sacrificed, my life broken, so—yes,' she agreed bitterly, 'let us both hope and pray that at least something good will come out of it.'

Chapter Five

She stood staring at the attractive little Temple of Nike,
its weathered stone golden in the sunlight. She had
made her way up to the Acropolis, knowing that she
would find a certain degree of peace despite the tourists
milling about, and the hoarse-throated guides, mainly
Greek women in dark clothes and carrying large hand-
bags, as if all their most precious possessions must be
carried with them. She caught the voice of one young
woman and listened automatically as she told of the
ancient custom of bringing a new robe to the goddess
Athena every four years. The procession must have
been magnificent, she mused, trying to picture the men
and maidens bringing the robe up to the Parthenon and
clothing the goddess in a ceremony which, though
pagan and primitive, was for all that carried out by a

people whose beliefs and customs had been instrumental in bringing civilisation to the western world—the whole world, as it was thought at that time, for no one had yet discovered the great lands across the sea.

Kathryn moved but forgot to be careful of the rough stones underfoot, the remains of columns fallen over the centuries and now lying sadly on the ground in a profusion of small pieces of weathered Pentellic marble. She cried out involuntarily as she twisted her ankle, and she would certainly have fallen had not strong arms come out and miraculously caught her even as she toppled forward.

'Oh,' she gasped, instinctively clinging to the young man's arm, 'thank you very much!'

'A pleasure.' He was English, tall, thin and boyish in appearance, with light grey eyes, a clear healthy skin and hair that had a touch of reddish-brown mingling with a lighter colour that was almost blond. 'These stones can be treacherous.'

'I ought to have taken more care. It isn't as if I haven't been here before.' Her ankle hurt when she put her weight on it, and noticing her wince, the young man gently led her over to a fallen column and urged her to sit down. The next moment he was holding her ankle, probing with strong but gentle fingers until, satisfied, he said there was no real damage but that a bruise was already appearing and, he said, she would suffer a little pain for a day or two.

'Are you on holiday?' he inquired after Kathryn had thanked him again.

'No, I live here.'

'In Athens?'

'Very close—yes, the actual address is Athens.'

'I live here, too.'

She looked surprised. 'I thought you might be a tourist,' she said, again taking in his appearance and this time including in her appraisal his clothes—an open-necked shirt of fine linen and well-cut pants of dark blue to contrast with the lighter colour of the shirt. He spoke in cultured accents, and she found herself asking curiously, 'Do you work here, then?'

He nodded, his eyes moving from her face to her throat, where he seemed to be interested in the delicate lines and the smooth hollows where the thin straps of her sun-top were white against the tan of her shoulders. A faint flush touched her cheeks at the undisguised admiration that lay in his roving glance.

'I'm a student at the hospital here, in Athens.' He paused, and when she made no comment, he went on interestedly, 'You live here, you say. Do you work in the city too?'

'No, I'm married. My husband's Greek and our house is here.' She spoke slowly and with a catch of which she was unconscious but which did not escape the man sitting beside her, his face turned to hers.

'You're young to be married,' he commented, and without thinking, she told him her age. 'You . . . er . . . sounded a little sad.' His hesitancy was obvious; it was a question, too, in a way, and Kathryn responded swiftly.

'I'm not sad. I've only been married a few weeks, so how can I be sad?' Again that catch in her voice, and she saw her companion's eyes take on a curious expression. He was going to be a doctor, so she surmised he was something of a psychologist, too. He would not have to be very clever, anyway, in order to see that she was not all joy, she told herself, trying to produce a smile in an attempt to erase the previous impression she had made. He responded to her smile, but the expression in his eyes was serious.

'Can I take you somewhere and we'll have afternoon tea?' he suggested, and Kathryn's hesitation lasted no more than a few seconds.

'That would be nice,' she returned, her smile deepening. 'I hadn't thought of it, but now you mention it, I realise I could do with a cup of tea.'

Together they went from the Acropolis to find a small *taverna* in the Plaka. It was high up, reached by several flights of twisting steps, but the climb was well worth it. The view over the Plaka and beyond was magnificent, with the sun's rays gilding the lovely temples, adding to their mellowness and seeming to add more magic, too, more mystery and even more beauty.

'Do you like living in Greece?' The young man put the question, but before she could answer, he told her his name.

She repeated it. 'Jake Pierce. Mine's Kathryn Coletis.'

'I like Kathryn. They call you Kate, I guess?"

'Some friends in England used to do, but my husband doesn't approve of its being shortened.' She was suddenly in a state of disturbed emotions and could not tell if it was the aftermath of the slight shock she had received when she jolted her ankle, or if it was fear that her husband would be furiously angry were he to know she was here taking afternoon tea with a strange young man . . . a very attractive young man, and English like herself. Leon would never approve. She had more than once told herself that he could be formidable if jealous. Yes, she supposed that he could be jealous even though he did not love her. She was his property according to the customs of Greece, and therefore she was not supposed to enjoy the company of any man other than her husband—at least, not alone, as she was at this moment.

She supposed it was inevitable that Jake should notice how she was, so she felt no surprise when, after the waiter had taken the order, then gone again, Jake said anxiously, 'Is something wrong, Kathryn? You look so troubled.'

'It isn't anything I can talk about,' she answered, but now she made no attempt to smile. On the contrary, a deep sigh accompanied her words. 'Tell me about your work,' she invited. 'Why are you here, instead of in England?'

He paused for a moment, fully aware of the reason why she had changed the subject. However, he talked for a few minutes while they waited to be served with their refreshments, and she learned that Jake had a great liking for Greece and its people and when the opportunity arose of his working in Athens, he had seized it without hesitation.

'And now—are you on holiday?'

'I have two weeks' vacation, yes. This is my first day.' There was a significance in that last short sentence, and Kathryn realised, not without a little shock, that she would not be averse to meething him now and then, just for a little break like the one she was having now. It was nice to be with one of her own people . . . and it also did something, however slight, to take her mind off the tragedy of her marriage.

'What are your plans?' she ventured. 'Are you staying in the city or going to one of the islands?'

'I shall stay in the capital. There's so much to see and explore. I'll leave the islands for another time.' He had an eagerness about him, and although he must be constantly aware of her being a married woman, there was an unmistakable invitation both in his eyes and in his voice. 'Do you come into town often?'

'I . . . I could do. . . .' She felt a pang of guilt even while telling herself she was not guilty of any serious crime.

'We could meet?'

He was bold, as a friend of Kathryn's from Ireland would have declared. It was a word which meant 'naughty' if said of a child, and 'forward' if said of an adult. She looked at him for a long moment before saying, 'We could, yes, Jake. Er . . . we could have afternoon tea here. I love this place.'

'So do I. I come here often—sometimes for lunch. It's relaxing because the tourists don't seem to have found it yet and so you have only the locals, people from offices or shops. They do a good lunch for less than two hundred drachmas.'

He was obviously inviting her to lunch with him. She said after a small silence, 'My husband is mostly at home for lunch, so I have it with him.'

'Mostly—but not always?'

Yes, he was bold—far too bold! 'My mother-in-law and sister-in-law live with us, and so even if my husband is not at home, they are.'

'And would wonder where you were if you did not have lunch with them?'

She swallowed hard, baffled by her emotions, by the tenseness within her. Had she already resigned herself to the possibility of her marriage coming to an end? Was it no longer of any importance in her life? Did her husband mean so little that she could think of escaping? Or was this desire to cultivate Jake's friendship born of a primitive wish for revenge for a hurt inflicted? She had always, basically, believed in an eye for an eye; she could not see why anyone should suffer a hurt or even a slight and not find a way to get even. It was fair. It was justice. Leon had wronged her grievously, so why should she not get her own back? He might, of course, never know, so what she was doing would not trouble him . . . but it would afford *her* a personal satisfaction and so she found herself saying, with a forced smile, 'I'm my own mistress. If I want to have my lunch out, then it has nothing to do with my husband's family.'

He glanced swiftly at her, and she knew she had gone too far to make a flat denial when Jake said, 'You're not happy, are you, Kathryn? Your marriage . . . well, you must admit you don't present a picture of the starry-eyed bride who's seeing nothing but roses and red wine before her.'

She passed her tongue over her lips. 'I don't want to talk about it, Jake.' And yet, before she had left him an hour and a half later, she had related the whole to him, allowing it to pour from her, unable to stop once she had begun, even though she would have wished to.

He left her and went on his way. They had arranged to meet the following day at the same time, same place—close to the Temple of Nike on the Acropolis.

It was after six o'clock when Kathryn arrived back at the villa. Leon was on the verandah, standing there as though he had been waiting for her. His first words, sharply spoken, strengthened the idea.

'Where have you been?' His dark eyes flashed over her figure and came to rest on her ankle, which was badly swollen.

'I went for a stroll.' She struggled and would have brushed past him, but he caught her wrist to halt her progress. She flared at the mastery of the action but said nothing, and after a moment he asked her where she had been strolling and what she had done to her foot.

'I was on the Acropolis, and I twisted my ankle by treading awkwardly on a stone.'

'It looks painful,' he observed. 'You'd better let me take a look at it.'

'There's no need,' coldly and with a tug to free herself, an attempt which failed. 'It's getting better on its own.'

'It's badly bruised.'

'That's nothing. I've had bruises before.'

Impatience lit her husband's eyes. 'Go inside,' he ordered peremptorily, 'and let me examine it. You might need to see the doctor.'

She set her teeth; her eyes met his in a challenge, but eventually she lowered them and obediently went into the house. Leon told her to sit down while he examined the ankle.

'Yes, it needs a doctor,' he decided, and she frowned at the top of his head and declared emphatically that she would not see a doctor.

'He'll only tell me to stay off it for several days, and I do not intend to do that.'

'You can go into the garden—'

'I want to go into town,' she snapped. 'I'm bored hanging around the house all day!'

'Bored?' he echoed, diverted and curious. 'This is the first time you have mentioned boredom. You've always said how much you enjoy the house and the grounds; you've enthused on the pleasure you get from Marina's company. This desire to go into town puzzles me, Kathryn.'

She faced him squarely as he let go of her foot and straightened up. 'Things were different then. After what I've learned, my life will be run on different lines. I feel that from now on I am my own mistress. You will go your way and I shall go mine.'

He was frowning heavily but it was puzzlement rather than anger that characterised his expression. 'What can you find to do in town?' he asked her slowly.

'There are the shops, the antiquities . . . oh, lots and lots to relieve the boredom.'

'Stop mentioning boredom,' he said harshly. 'And you can just stop all this other nonsense. We're married, and it's as a married couple we shall live—'

'No!' she broke in fiercely. 'We shall not live as

married people! I refuse to be a wife to a man who does not love me!'

The dark, serpentine eyes narrowed to mere slits. 'Am I to understand that our marriage is to be platonic from now on?' There was the hint of an amused sneer in his tone, which only served to ignite her anger, although her voice was quiet enough when she answered him.

'Yes, it is, Leon. Marriage without love is something I had not envisaged. You were in the wrong entirely, and I was duped—the poor trusting fool whom no doubt you were laughing at! Well, as I've already said, you're going to pay!'

He glowered down at her, but she met his threatening eyes unflinchingly because she held all the aces.

'And if I am not in agreement?' he said in a softly dangerous tone of voice. 'If I insist on my rights?'

'Rights?' with a glint of challenge in her eye. 'What rights do you happen to have, might I ask?'

She heard him grit his teeth. 'I'm your husband!'

'You are, I agree, but as you married me under false pretenses, you have no rights—as you like to term them!'

'We can't go through life in the way you are contemplating—' he began, but she interrupted him.

'If you think I shall agree to a divorce, you are mistaken! If you want Eugenia, then you will have to take her as your mistress!'

'You . . . !' Leon took a step towards her, then stopped, as she thrust out her hands in a defensive gesture. 'Kathryn, don't try me too far. You've only seen one side of me, but I assure you there's another, and it's very different. Take my word for it and be warned!'

She paled a little, and her nerves began to play up. Her temper flared as a result and she decided to use one of her aces. 'If you do not promise to leave me alone, then I shall not give the ring to your sister.' She did not mean it, but hoped she had been sufficiently convincing, and watching his changed expression, she breathed a little sigh of satisfaction and relief.

His face was almost as pale as hers as he said, the words coming from between clenched teeth, 'You'd punish my sister—sacrifice her happiness?'

'Mine was sacrificed—remember?' Kathryn thought of the happy days when she had her job and the flat and she and Carole used to tend the garden lovingly. She recalled happy hours spent at the seminars at Branton Manor just down the road. Peaceful, trouble-free days spreading into months and no problems coming along except the minor ones of an unexpectedly large electric bill or a repair needed for the car. No heartache or dissension . . . no husband who did not love her. She thought: Women do not know when they are well-off. They all want more than anything to get married, because nature meant them to mate and reproduce, but with marriage comes the problems. . . . No, that was not a fair conclusion. It was not justifiable to judge all marriages on the failure of her own.

'I can't really believe you'd keep the ring . . .' Leon broke off, then added, with a surprising edge of capitulation to his tone, 'I cannot take the risk. You have my promise.'

She stared, numbed, and with an almost physical

pain in the region of her heart. She wondered if he guessed that this was not really what she wanted. But what *did* she want? She could not let him make love to her, knowing as she did that not only had he no love for her but that he was in love with someone else. In her agony she could easily imagine him pretending it was Eugenia he was making love to. . . .

'I hope you will keep your promise,' she said in a low tone.

'I shall certainly try,' was all he said, and she sent him a swift and rather frightened glance.

'I want it categorically,' she began, but he shook his head.

'I'm human, Kathryn,' he reminded her, and his manner and expression were almost tender. 'I might slip—I cannot say with certainty that I can always resist my lovely wife.'

She stared again, and tears gathered to dim her eyes. He looked so sad, so lost in distress, that her soft heart went out to him and it was with the greatest difficulty that she stopped herself from going to him and pulling his head onto her breast. 'Shall we try to make a go of it?' she wanted to ask. 'Can you ever come to care for me? If so, then I can let you make love to me. . . .' The words would never come. For if they did, Leon would be in a most embarrassing position; he would have to tell her he could never love her because he loved someone else. Yet . . . he had said all was over between him and his old flame. . . . But he would have to say that, mused Kathryn. Yes, he would have to say that to the woman who was his wife.

She was sure, though, that it wasn't true.

She looked at her husband and said quietly, 'If you ever do break your promise, Leon, then I shall leave you.' And with that she walked painfully to the door and opened it. 'And I don't want the doctor,' she said over her shoulder. 'My ankle hurts, but there's no real damage done to it.'

Chapter Six

Dust spiraled up from behind the car as Leon drove away from the villa. He had lost his temper when she had insisted on going out for lunch. He himself had an appointment with a business associate but had expected Kathryn to lunch with his mother and Marina.

'I'm lunching out,' Kathryn had told him firmly, and her husband had frowned and demanded to know why it was so important for her to go out.

'It isn't as if you have anyone to meet,' he had asserted, and at that she had fluttered her long lashes, bringing them down to hide her expression.

'What does that signify?' she had countered. 'I enjoy the city; it's exciting, full of life. There is no life here!' Derisive the tone and the look she gave him. These assertions she repeatedly made were far from true, but she wanted to hurt him; in fact, the desire to hurt him had become almost an obsession.

'It's the third time this week you've been out for lunch!'

'And tomorrow will be the fourth.' It was at that juncture that Leon had lost his temper, warning her not to test his patience too far because he would not be responsible for his reaction if she did. 'Lay a finger on me and I shall leave you,' she had threatened, and now, with tears misting her vision, she watched the car speeding along the drive, a wrathful man at the wheel. She turned as her mother-in-law came silently onto the patio.

Their eyes met and held for a long intense moment before the older woman broke it to say, 'You've quarrelled, dear?'

'It's nothing. Just one of those tiffs . . .' She trailed to silence, her voice caught by the painful constriction in her throat. She turned away, unwilling to let Mrs. Coletis see the tears in her eyes.

'I see there are problems,' insisted Mrs. Coletis. 'It was only to be expected.'

'I don't understand?'

'Leon told me you had overheard a conversation between Marina and me.'

'I see. . . .' She supposed it was not unnatural that Leon would mention the matter, probably with both anger and regret. 'Does Marina know about it?'

'No, and we don't want her to.'

'I can understand that.'

'We don't want any setbacks. Leon says you are giving Marina the ring tomorrow, on her birthday.'

'That's right.'

'You believe in the curse?' curiously and after a small pause.

'I didn't—until I met your son!'

'Kathryn, dear—'

'Mrs. Coletis, please accept that I am not in the mood to discuss the situation between Leon and me!'

'You would call me Mrs. Coletis? You were calling me *matera*.'

'If I do not regard Leon as my husband, then I can scarcely regard you as my mother.' She was still turned away, avoiding the possibility of revealing her tears. They had fallen onto her cheeks, and surreptitiously she brushed a hand across them as she said, 'You'll have to excuse me, Mrs. Coletis. I am going out for lunch.'

'You don't wish any longer to share lunch with Marina and me?' Sad the tone, and Kathryn bit her lip. She liked her mother-in-law enormously and felt sorry for her, too, because she could have had such a good life with Demetrius if it hadn't been for her daughter's illness.

'I like to get away from this house,' was all she said when at length she broke the silence. 'I'm so disillusioned, as I know you would be if you were in my position.'

She left the patio, and the woman standing there—a tall and elegant woman looking years younger than her age, which was fifty-five. She took care of her hair and her skin; she dressed with extraordinary taste and *chic*. It was no wonder Demetrius was in love with her. And how patient and understanding he was! Kathryn felt that all these people were fine and likable, and if only her marriage had been normal, she could have been the happiest girl in the world. As it was . . . well, she seemed to have a subconscious desire to dislike anyone and everyone who had anything to do with her husband, which, she honestly owned, was not only illogical but also unfair and very mean-minded.

But how did one cope with such emotions? Her feelings towards both Mrs. Coletis and her daughter had become negative—although she would never have done either of them harm. She especially had sympathy for Marina, whose illness—whether caused by the curse or not—was most distressing, and when Kathryn had met Christos one day when he called unexpectedly to see Marina, she had felt inexpressibly sad for them both. It was plain that the young man was madly in love with Marina, but he still had this other friend. Kathryn, finding herself alone with him for a moment, had tentatively asked him about her. He was in no way serious, he had said. She was merely his mistress, and if he could not marry Marina, then he would continue to have this girl, but she knew he would never make her his wife.

She met Jake at a pre-arranged place in the Plaka and they decided to drive to a restaurant at Glifadha which Jake had frequented when he first came to Athens a few years ago on holiday. They sat in a shady garden and looked out over the smooth, aquamarine sea where caiques and graceful yachts and other vessels provided their own special interest.

'What are you having?' Jake's voice was low, familiar, his smile spontaneous, his eyes frank and open. 'I expect you are starting with a *mezé?*'

She nodded, opening up the menu and soon deciding on the *souvlaki*—lamb roasted on a charcoal grill and flavoured with thyme and other herbs. It was served on a skewer and had as accompaniments crisp fried potatoes and a fresh green salad. The wind which Jake chose was Domestika, product of the Peloponnese, where, in the Middle Ages, the Crusaders from France cultivated vineyards which had produced the wine ever since.

But first came the starter, a *mezé* of aubergines marinated in oil, pistachio nuts, small pieces of *anguri* —which were the delicious small cucumbers so popular everywhere in Greece—and several kinds of small fish roe topped with caviar.

'That was delicious!' enthused Kathryn, wondering how, in so short a time, she had come to like Jake so much. He was charming, thoughtful, attentive. . . . All a woman could desire in an escort. That he liked her was more than evident; in fact, there was already danger because, aware as he was of the failure of her marriage, he had not put too much restraint on his feelings and it was evident to Kathryn that he would need very little encouragement to speak openly of her attraction for him.

The wine came; it was delicious and a little heady.

'I shall be on air in a moment.' She laughed as she spread a hand above her glass when he would have filled it up. 'You can manage the rest surely?'

'Have a drop more,' he persuaded. 'Just a little drop.'

But she shook her head. 'I have to go home, remember.'

'And it wouldn't do for your husband to see you tipsy.'

'Well, he'd guess I'd not managed to get that way on my own.'

He was serious for a moment, looking at her with the undisguised admiration to which she was fast becoming used. 'Does it really matter if he knows about us?'

There, it was out! Kathryn had not wanted it to be like this. She was happy with Jake, seeing him every day, either for lunch or afternoon tea, and with never a thought for anything beyond the present. She was in limbo, sad at heart and trying this form of escapism in order to assuage both the pain and her pride.

'I don't want a showdown,' she said frankly. 'You see, Jake, I still love my husband—'

'You can't, dear, not after what he did to you,' protested Jake, automatically passing her a menu which had just been handed to him. She accepted it, but said immediately that she did not want a dessert, just coffee—French coffee, not the sticky black concoction called Turkish coffee. 'You can't still love him,' repeated Jake on accepting the menu back again. 'Such a revelation must surely have killed your love.'

But she shook her head, and saw him fix his eyes on the thick halo of her hair as it shone with the movement, catching the sun's slanting rays as they escaped through the branches of the trees.

'You don't let love die so easily, Jake. Much as it hurts here . . .' She put a quivering hand to her left breast. 'Much as it hurts, you don't let it die.'

'You'd like it to, though?' he asked, and a frown creased her wide, intelligent brow.

'I suppose it would be more comfortable,' she admitted. 'But what a loss.'

'One should cut one's losses and start again, Kathryn.' So solemn and persistent. She said gently, automatically lifting her glass and regarding him from above its rim, 'You have a lot of studying to do, Jake, before you can think of anything else.'

'Marriage?' He sighed, and for a space there was silence between them. 'I want you for my friend—and for always, Kathryn,' he stated when at last he spoke.

'Let us not talk about such things, but take what we have,' she begged. 'I'm happy with you, Jake, but I don't love you. A woman can love only one man at a time,' she added with a feeble little laugh.

'I think you could come to care—'

'Please,' she entreated swiftly. 'Don't spoil what we have, Jake.'

He let the matter drop, much to her relief, but when the meal was over, he asked her if she really had to go back or if she could stay with him a little while longer. Because the temptation to be happy was strong, she consented and they walked on the seafront, Kathryn as always affected deeply by the invigorating air, said to be unique in all the world. It seemed to stimulate one's thoughts and ideas, one's energies, even. And one never craved for food in this climate, which was unusual; Kathryn had once remarked to her husband that the air was a substitute for food.

'Happy?' Jake took her hand, and she did not resist. His glance was slanting, admiring, anxious. 'You sometimes look so sad, dear, and it makes me sad too.'

'I am sad at times,' she admitted. 'I was so optimistic about my marriage, and yet . . .'

'Yes?'

'I knew so little about Leon. We had three weeks together while on holiday, and then he asked me to marry him.'

'If he lives here, then why was he on holiday for three weeks in Greece? I mean, you'd have supposed he'd go somewhere a bit farther afield than the Peloponnese.'

'He wasn't on holiday originally. He admitted this later. He'd had some business meeting at the hotel and another one somewhere else, so he stayed on for a couple of days or, rather, that was his original intention. But then he saw the ring and decided to try to get it.' She paused, reluctant to discuss her husband, but then she remembered she had told Jake just about everything anyway, so it did not matter if he knew the rest.

'He actually told you all this?' Jake was plainly puzzled at the idea of Leon's making such an admission.

'Not until later. When I asked him how he came to be in the Peloponnese for three weeks, he said at first that he was so attracted to me that he just had to stay. However, it wasn't that at all.'

'This ring seems really to be cursed,' he said after a thoughtful silence.

115

'It's the whole set of jewellery, not just one piece.'

'You believe in it?'

'I don't know, Jake. It's a very strange business. I never was one to believe in the supernatural, but undoubtedly there's something a little frightening about this jewellery.'

'Why the dickens didn't Marina sell it?'

'I feel she would have done, but it was a present from her father and she felt sentimental about it. Don't forget, she didn't have the illness until she learned about the curse.'

'Which proves it's psychological.'

'That's what my husband says, but he felt the only way to make Marina better was to get that ring for her.'

'I still think that he ought to have persuaded her to sell it.'

Kathryn shook her head, remembering Leon's saying that Marina had at first been secretive and so neither he nor his mother had even remotely guessed that the illness stemmed from imaginings due to Marina's knowledge of the curse.

'It was too late anyway. She is genuinely ill, Jake.'

'I don't doubt it, but it's a most interesting case from a doctor's point of view. The girl's own doctors can't help her, of course.'

'They can't diagnose the complaint, so they're helpless.'

'I wonder if she'll improve after you've given her the ring.'

'We're all hoping so, especially her young man. He's so nice, Jake, and he's very much in love with her.'

Jake fell silent, and for a while they strolled along in a

companionable quietness with only the song of birds and chirping of cicadas to intrude. Palms danced against a clear sapphire sky and the scent of flowers filled the air. The sun was hot, but a faint breeze came in from the sea, bringing a welcome coolness to fan their faces. Kathryn was happy in a certain way even while poignantly aware of memories . . . lovely memories of walks like this by the sea at Nauplia, walks with the man she loved. . . . She remembered the delightful little cafés strung along the waterfront where you could take afternoon tea and face the clear shining waters of the bay. The cafés were often set under a canopy of vines or beneath shady trees, and flowers seemed to abound everywhere. Happy days, but the memories had now become sad.

After a while she glanced at her watch. 'I really must ask you to drive me back,' she said, but with a sigh which could not possibly escape her companion.

'It isn't so very late,' he began, but she shook her head, repeating that it was time he drove her back.

They drove in silence for most of the way, absorbed in their own thoughts. But as they entered the bustle of the city, he asked if he could drive her home.

'Right home?' she exclaimed. 'No, Jake—'

'I didn't mean right to your very door. But at least I can drop you within walking distance.'

He had never even suggested this before, but in any case, this was the first time they had gone out of the city. Usually they lunched in the Plaka or in one of the hotels.

'All right,' she agreed after another moment's thought. 'You can drop me near the main road. There's a small road off it, and then our drive branches out through the trees.'

In recent years Athens had spread high up into the foothills near the massive amphitheatre on the heights, and wealthy people had settled in these cooler places where the scenery and panoramic views were unparallelled for their beauty. And it was on one of these wooded slopes that Leon's father had built the luxurious villa, set in several lush acres of gardens and woodland. It was an idyllic setting and yet close to the city.

'This is where you can drop me,' Kathryn said when, at length, Jake turned off the main road onto a smaller one lined with palms and jacaranda trees with here and there a crimson hibiscus flaunting its glorious blooms in the sunshine.

'Tomorrow?' Jake asked briefly and with a sideways glance as he stopped the car.

'Where shall we meet?'

'Constitution Square.' He told her exactly where he would be, and then he got out of the car, went to her side and opened the door for her to alight. And as she came close to where he was standing, he brushed her cheek with his lips.

She coloured and shied away . . . and yet she had known, somehow, that he would kiss her today. . . .

'Till tomorrow, then. Noon, as usual.'

She stood for a while watching the car before turning to walk along the smaller road, which was really not a road at all but merely a track wide enough for one car only. It had a couple of passing places which were scarcely necessary, as the only cars to use the track were those belonging to Leon and another property owner who lived some few hundred yards farther along.

She walked slowly, her thoughts flitting from Jake to Leon and back again. She was not conducting her life very well at all, she concluded, feeling the wisest thing she could do would be to break with Jake without any further delay. And yet, if she did, what was there to live for? Bitterly it was borne in upon her that she was in a sorry plight if all she had to live for were these clandestine meetings with a man she did not even love. A deep sigh escaped her as she thought of Jake and the way he was beginning to care for her. It certainly was not fair to him, this rapidly developing affair. Yes, it was an affair, even though there was nothing seriously wrong taking place. She had not been unfaithful to her husband and she never would be. Her ideals were still high and she was thankful that with the changes that were taking place within her, at least she had not damaged her honour. But what of the future? Leon had taught her things about herself which she had never known, or even guessed. He had brought about the discovery that she was a passionate woman with desires which were equal to his. They had been perfectly matched physically, but now she seemed to be facing a future of cold isolation from all that was natural between a man and a woman. A starved life, barren and lonely. Tears gathered; she brushed them away, angry at her weakness of self-pity.

It was the life she herself had chosen, having rejected her husband, so she could do nothing but abide by the decision she had made. But this brought her no nearer the vital decision of whether or not to break with Jake. She decided to leave it for a while, since he would be back at the hospital within a few days, working hard and therefore unable to see her very often. Yes, she would leave it for a while—let things develop in their own way.

The house was warm and welcoming in the golden light of the Grecian sun, and for a moment Kathryn's heart was strangely light. This was her home and could be for as long as she cared to live here. She was fortunate in some ways. But as she drew closer, her heart became heavy again, because she wanted to see her husband come lovingly to meet her, to take her in his arms. . . .

'You've been gone a long time!' he said harshly when, on entering the hall, she came face to face with him. 'What do you do by yourself for several hours every day?'

'Look at the shops,' she answered and, sweeping past him, she went to her room, there to put her face in her hands and weep bitterly into them.

Chapter Seven

The following evening there was a special dinner for Marina's birthday. Kathryn had given her the ring that morning, and she felt she would never ever forget the glowing look on her sister-in-law's face as she held it in her hand for a long moment before slipping it onto her little finger.

'How can I thank you, dearest Kathryn?' Marina's eyes shone up at her from the chair in which she was sitting—not the wheelchair, for she used that only when she wanted to get about the house and garden, but a chair by the window where, on a small table, her breakfast had been placed by one of the maids. Kathryn had gone in to her private little sitting-room and had presented her with the ring. It had been strange, giving it away, and for a while Kathryn had known a tinge of resentment at having to part with it. Yet hadn't she always said she would be glad if she ever found the owner of the rest of the jewellery? 'You have no idea what this means to me,' she heard Marina say eagerly. 'I never thought you would make me this lovely gift. I shall treasure it forever!'

Kathryn stood staring down at her. 'You're going to wear it all the time?'

'Of course—for a while at any rate.' There was a long pause, and Kathryn strongly suspected that Marina came very near to telling her the story of the curse. However, Marina merely said, 'I feel so happy, Kathryn! And I am really looking forward to my party this evening!'

'Party?' It was the first Kathryn had heard of a party. 'Are you having one?'

'Well, it's not really a party, but a dinner for six of us.'

'Six? I suppose Demetrius is coming, but who is the other one?'

'Christos,' supplied Marina quietly. 'I feel so happy that he will be with us.'

Christos and Kathryn had sat together in the salon where aperitifs were taken while they waited for the signal that dinner was ready. Kathryn had said curiously, 'If Marina gets better, you'll marry her?'

'But of course.' He was a man of medium height with very dark skin and eyes. He was very English, though, in his looks, in the clean-cut structure of his face, and he spoke with scarcely any accent at all.

'You believe she will get better?'

'I pray for it, Kathryn,' he answered seriously. 'It is a

strange illness which came slowly but frightened me as I watched my beloved become morose and sad, as if she had some secret trouble on her mind that was eating into it, and into her body.'

He paused, and Kathryn said with a frown, 'Did you not feel it was a remarkable thing that the doctors—obviously the best obtainable—could not discover what had caused this illness?'

'It baffled everyone because Marina was so full of life. I loved her on sight and would have married her very soon, but I had my studies to finish—I was at Athens University. Well, this malady came . . .' He broke off, spreading his hands in a little gesture of helplessness and bafflement. 'It is still a mystery and always will be, whether she recovers or not.'

Obviously he knew nothing about the curse, and Kathryn could not help wondering what he would think if he ever did learn of it. He was so practical that she felt he would never believe that such things could be effective . . . and yet it had been effective. But only because Marina was susceptible to such things, being superstitious.

'Perhaps you won't have to wait long for Marina to get better.' Kathryn's glance strayed to the girl who was in the wheelchair, talking to her brother and appearing to be in very earnest conversation. How lovely she was, with her gleaming black hair and those beautiful big eyes, expressive eyes, widely spaced and framed by the longest lashes Kathryn had ever seen. She was animated, more alive than Kathryn had ever seen her before, and Kathryn had no regrets at having parted with the ring.

It was a week later that Marina said she wanted to get out of the chair and walk. Kathryn was with her, walking beside the chair, but at the girl's request she stopped dead and stared down at her in disbelief.

'You . . . you . . . believe you c-can walk . . : on your own?'

'I want to try. You are with me, dear Kathryn, and will see that I don't fall.'

But Kathryn shook her head emphatically. 'I'll go and fetch Leon,' she promised, and before the girl could protest, she sped away, her heart beating over-rate at the idea of the girl asking to walk after only a week! It was frightening— Her thoughts were cut off as, before she had even reached the patio—from where she would have entered the house—Leon appeared, staring past her. As she turned, she saw Marina standing by the chair, holding the handles tightly for support.

Leon ran towards her, with Kathryn following at a slower pace. 'Marina!' His voice echoed over the garden, stern and imperious. 'What are you doing?'

'I am all right, Leon. I felt stronger yesterday and the day before, so I decided that today, if I felt stronger still, I'd try to walk a little. Will you please hold on to me? I asked Kathryn, but she looked so frightened and ran away to get you.'

He turned, and his eyes met those of his wife. There was a tense, electric atmosphere around them, as if each were asking the other if they really believed in this miracle. Leon was the one to break the silence, but he spoke to his sister as, moving close, he extended his hand. The next moment they were walking slowly across the grass, with Kathryn staring after them and mentally rejecting what was so visible before her eyes. She recalled vividly the professor's attitude towards the curse; he had an open mind, he said, refusing to pass it off as nonsense.

'Kathryn, I can walk.' Then there was a cry of pain, and if Leon had not caught Marina in his arms, she would have collapsed. Kathryn ran to her, horror in her eyes. Marina was in pain, and she was sobbing piteously. Leon's face was grey and grim.

'I ought not to have allowed it,' he rasped, striding away across the lawn with his sister in his arms. The doctor was sent for and shook his head as he came away.

'As I told you before, Leon, your sister . . .' His voice trailed off and he stopped speaking. Puzzled, Kathryn looked at her husband . . . and knew that with a glance he had prevented the doctor's revealing something, something Leon had obviously not wanted her to hear.

'Marina's been feeling so much better lately,' remarked Leon. 'I always believed her illness was psychological and that one day she would throw off this mysterious illness.'

'And you thought the time had come now?'

'Yes, I did.' Yet as Kathryn looked at him, she felt sure he had no belief in the adverse effects of the curse. He believed that Marina had been improving only because, having obtained possession of the ring, *she* believed it was the panacea for her illness.

'But I did insist that there was some disease of the bones.'

'Yes, Phidas,' impatiently and with a growing frown. 'But neither you nor any of the other specialists could give any sort of a satisfactory diagnosis.'

The doctor merely gave that expressive shrug and left a few minutes later. Leon and Kathryn exchanged glances. It had all been for nothing, they were telling one another. *There was no curse on the jewellery.* Marina's illness was not psychological, but was purely medical, but obviously of a kind which, as yet, was practically unknown.

'I'll go and sit with her,' decided Kathryn in a flat, lifeless tone. 'I don't suppose I can make her cheer up, but at least I can offer comfort.'

Leon's face was grim in the shafting sunlight spraying the room; Kathryn saw his mouth move convulsively before he said, in a voice hoarse with sadness and emotion, 'Thank you, Kathryn.'

She hesitated, wanting desperately to comfort him as well, to go to him and put her arms about him, to kiss away the grim sadness of his mouth. All she did was to walk slowly to the door and say over her shoulder, 'I'll stay for about an hour, and then I think you should come, Leon. Marina loves you very much, and she'll expect you. And I suppose, meanwhile, that you will tell your mother what has happened?'

'I don't look forward to doing so, but, yes, it will have to be done.'

Kathryn went out and closed the door softly behind her. Mrs. Coletis was at the hairdresser's; she little knew what was awaiting her when she returned in half an hour or so.

'So you are not going out to town?' Leon asked the question a few days later when, on passing the open door of the dining-room, he turned back, having seen Kathryn arranging flowers for the table.

'No, not today.' Her voice was coolly impersonal and she turned away after the one brief meeting of her eyes with his.

She sensed his rising anger, but his voice retained a quality of calm as he said, 'So you'll be having lunch with your family?'

'*My* family?'

'Whatever you like to think to the contrary, you are married to me and, therefore, you have a family.'

'I have never said I'm not married to you.'

'You know what I mean!' Rasping the voice now, as his anger seeped through the veneer he had endeavoured to place over it. 'You're my wife—in every sense!'

'It's a sham. From your point of view it was a marriage of convenience, and until that disastrous occurrence of a few days ago, it was likely to have had its bright side. Your sister would have recovered and been married to a man she loves—and *who loves her!*' She laughed without humour and turned to him, 'I would then have seen something for the wreckage of my life, wouldn't I? I'd have seen your sister happily married!'

'Stop being bitter. I've already said, you don't know everything.'

127

'Now's your chance to tell me, then.' She took a rose in her fingers and caressed the velvet petals almost tenderly.

Leon watched her broodingly for a while before saying unexpectedly, 'Will you ever forgive me, Kathryn?'

'Forgive?' She had never expected him to ask a thing like that. His pride—what had happened to it? 'No,' she stated emphatically at last, 'I shall never forgive you—never as long as I live!'

He seemed to turn grey about the mouth, and there was certainly no mistaking the brooding dejection in his eyes. He seemed to be hurt, yet how could he be, seeing that he did not love her? Perhaps it was a pose, an act designed to soften her so that she would forgive him and then he could use her again, this time in another way . . . as a convenience. He would come to her and make love to her. It would save him having a pillow-friend, for she guessed he would not be able to continue the saintly life much longer. Well, let him have his pillow-friend. He could have a dozen, for all she cared!

'You won't forgive me, and yet you love me?' Leon sighed and shook his head, and again Kathryn was struck by this lowering of his pride. 'It's a very strange attitude to take—'

'Strange?' she flashed. 'It's the only attitude to take. And as for my loving you . . .' She stopped to let her eyes rove over him in comptempt. 'I did once, but not now! Do you suppose I could love a man who treated me as you have done?'

'You don't love me?' His voice was as sceptical as his glance. 'I can understand your pride, Kathryn—'

'Pride doesn't come into it. I do not love you, get that!' She prayed that she was convincing in the lie which had come to her unbidden. She had stated so strongly that pride did not come into it, but it must surely have been pride that forced her to say she no longer loved him. With a heavy heart she watched his expression and knew without any doubt at all that he believed her, believed she had lost the love she had had for him in the beginning.

'In that case,' he said slowly and resignedly, 'that's all there is to it.'

'I hope you consider it was all worthwhile—but of course you do. Marina will get better and, after all, Marina's welfare is well worth the wreckage you've made of my life, isn't it?'

Anger had brought bright colour to her cheeks, but inside . . . Why did she want to hurt him?—if the word 'hurt' could apply. She was hurting herself more, bringing a pain to her heart that was almost physical.

'I feel this bitterness will pass one day,' her husband commented in quiet, almost gentle accents. 'You're not the kind of girl to harbour it forever.' And with that he swung around on his heels and left her, the rose in her hand, its delicate perfume in her nostrils. She put it in the vase, unable to see what she was doing because the tears had filled her eyes, blinding them.

She left the dining room and went to her bedroom, then into the bathroom, where she ran warm water into the hand basin and dabbed her eyes, then dried them on the towel. Her mind was confused, because all she could think about was her husband's assertion that she did not know everything—and it was the second time he'd said it. She had invited him to explain, but he had ignored her and changed the subject. What was there for her to know? Perhaps he was merely saying that, trying to make excuses for his conduct; but there were no excuses.

During the afternoon, Jake telephoned. Kathryn had told him what time to do so—a time when she knew Leon always went for a walk—and as she heard his voice, her heart immediately became light. Fate had sent her this young man, she mused, and at this moment she could easily have left the villa and gone to him.

But the feeling soon passed, and she heard herself say, in answer to his invitation to have lunch with him the following day, 'That'll be nice, Jake. Shall I meet you in the usual place—in Constitution Square?'

'I shall be there!'

'You sound exceedingly happy.'

'I've just taken an exam and know I've passed.'

'Congratulations. It must be a wonderful feeling to come from the examination room and know you've done a good job.'

'It is a wonderful feeling. I'm on air! And so tomorrow, dear, we shall have a bottle of champagne to celebrate.'

'At lunchtime? Champagne's for dinner.'

'But you and I can't have dinner together.'

'No. . . .'

'Or can we?' His tone was persuasive . . . and the suggestion was tempting!

Yet she hesitated, for it would be going rather too far to be away from home at dinnertime. 'I'll think about it,' she promised. 'Meanwhile, I'll meet you tomorrow at noon.'

'I'll be there. Good-bye, Kathryn.'

'Good-bye, Jake.'

She replaced the receiver slowly and thoughtfully. This could not continue indefinitely, and yet she would have a bleak prospect in front of her if she gave Jake up. Nothing to look forward to. She felt she would be forced to leave, to return to her own country and try to pick up the threads again. But her lovely flat was gone and she would never ever get one quite like it again. Her job, too, had been rather special; she could never hope to find another quite as pleasantly interesting and with the kind of boss who never complained or asked too much of his employees.

So much lost, and what for? It served her right for rushing into marriage with a man she scarcely knew. Why, she felt she knew Jake almost as well as she had known Leon when she married him!

Jake. . . . She had to keep in mind that he was becoming far too fond of her, that with only the slightest encouragement he would suggest they have an affair. But she knew that it would not in his case be for any other reason than that he cared. . . .

She wandered out into the garden and was soon

joined by her mother-in-law. One glance at the older woman's pale, anxious face brought forth the question, 'Is something wrong, Mrs. Coletis?'

'I was just picking up my telephone when your friend rang.'

It was Kathryn's turn to lose colour. 'You . . . heard?'

'Everything.' The older woman, immaculate as always, with not a hair out of place, looked at her with neither censure nor contempt, but with pain in her eyes, deep pain and sadness. 'You're obviously having an affair—'

'It depends what you mean by having an affair!' Kathryn broke in swiftly. 'I have done nothing to be ashamed of, Mrs. Coletis.'

'You're seeing this young man—this Jake—when you go out. I suspected something, because it wasn't natural for you to be wandering about the streets of Athens alone so much. But I tried to shake off my suspicions.' She looked directly at Kathryn. 'I hope you know the risk you take. My son has a side to his nature that even I would not wish to see too often.'

'He's seeing Eugenia.'

'What makes you say that?'

'Christos saw them together, remember?'

'It's a great pity you overheard Marina and me speaking that day.'

'It was as well for me, Mrs. Coletis,' returned Kathryn coldly. 'I was living in a fool's paradise, whereas now I have come down to earth and my feet are firmly on the ground. You say that Leon has this other side to his nature, but that does not trouble me.

He dare not touch me, for if he did, then I would leave him.'

The older woman winced. 'You've told him this?'

'He knows just how I feel, and that I stay here only to suit myself. If ever he does anything to hurt or even annoy me, then it will no longer suit me to stay, and I shall go.'

'My dear Kathryn . . .' Mrs. Coletis came close and touched her arm. 'You've been dreadfully hurt, but Leon did treat you kindly, and I am sure that if you had not so unfortunately overheard what you did, you'd never have known that Leon did not love you.' The voice was quiet and gentle and somehow pleading, as well.

'I know all this.' Kathryn shook her head in a negative gesture. 'I'd have discovered it one day simply because a woman has this natural intuition; she senses things, and I know without any doubt at all that I would have sensed, eventually, that Leon did not love me.'

The older woman's glance was strange as she said, 'Were I you, with your looks and charm, I'd accept this situation as a challenge.'

'What do you mean?'

It was a few seconds before her mother-in-law spoke, for her attention had been arrested by two dainty little geckos who were chasing one another across the fine low-cut grass of the lawn. When presently she did speak, it was to say, 'I'd set about making my husband fall in love with me.'

Kathryn's chin lifted. 'Run after him? Flirt with him? Is that what you mean?'

'Sort of.' There was a faint smile of amusement on

her lips as she added, 'After all, you of the West have this thing called women's liberation, which, I gather, gives you the right to be on equal terms with men. Therefore you are quite within your rights to pursue a man and to go on pursuing until he's caught.'

Somehow, that was so amusing, coming from a woman like Mrs. Coletis, who was always so correct and proper, that Kathryn actually found herself laughing. But she soon became serious again as she said that although she believed in women's lib and equality, she certainly did not intend 'chasing' her husband in order to make him fall in love with her. It had been done before, was Mrs. Coletis' swift reminder, but Kathryn merely shook her head in dismissal of the idea.

'In any case, Leon would hate that,' she ended thoughtfully.

'He wouldn't know, not if you are clever.'

Again Kathryn shook her head, but now she was actually musing on the older woman's suggestion. And it came as something of a shock to realise that she was actually considering it—not dismissing it, throwing it out, but accepting it as a possibility.

After all, Leon was attracted to her in one way. . . . Could she create an interest that was spiritual, as well? Suddenly the idea became exciting, a challenge, as Mrs. Coletis had said it would be if she were in Kathryn's place.

'You . . . you really believe I could make Leon fall in love with me?' she asked unsteadily. And then she added with a frown, 'What about this Eugenia? I heard Marina say he was in love with her.'

A wise little smile came to Mrs. Coletis' lips and

hovered there while she looked at her daughter-in-law, taking in the silken mass of honey-brown hair, the big eyes beneath delicate brows, the small well-shaped nose and the wide generous mouth. 'My dear,' she murmured at length, 'if my son had been in love with Eugenia—really in love—do you suppose he could have hurt her by marrying another woman, no matter how pressing the reason?'

'He loves his sister,' was the evasive reply, and now there *was* a hint of censure on Mrs. Coletis' face.

'I asked you a question, dear, and you evaded an answer. Can it be that you are reluctant to give even an inch?'

Kathryn averted her head, profoundly aware of the fact that her mother-in-law had hit the nail on the head. She, Kathryn, was being antagonistic to a degree that could lead to her own destruction, for there was nothing to prevent Leon, should he come to the end of his patience, from demanding a divorce—which he could get on the grounds that she was not being a proper wife to him—after which he could marry Eugenia if he so wished. Or perhaps another woman. . . . The thought of Leon being married to anyone else was so unbearable that Kathryn thrust the picture out, refusing to allow it to remain in her mental vision a moment longer.

She heard her mother-in-law give a little cough, and this brought her back to the question which had been asked. Kathryn looked at her and said curiously, 'Are you saying that Leon was not really in love with Eugenia?'

Mrs. Coletis paused a moment, as if she were

considering an answer. 'I'll not deny that he liked her a lot at one time,' she was honest enough to say. 'However, I feel that he could never have been deeply in love or he'd never have sacrificed her happiness, and his own at the same time.'

'Is she beautiful?' An irrelevant question, and one that brought another smile to her mother-in-law's lips.

'Very, my dear, but in a dramatically different way from you.'

A moment's hesitation, and then, shyly, 'Do you think . . . think that Leon would ever fall in love with me . . . if . . . I tried . . . as you suggest?'

'I believe you have a rather more than ordinary chance of success.'

'I wouldn't know how to begin—'

'Nonsense, Kathryn,' admonished her mother-in-law. 'From the time of Eden, woman has managed to ensnare her man—'

'Oh, I don't like your putting it like that!' flashed Kathryn with a touch of anger. 'It sounds primitive and . . . and scheming.'

'Of course it's primitive and scheming,' admitted the older woman mildly. 'But what's wrong with the primitive? We've come too far from it; that's what is wrong with the world today.' She stopped, waiting for some comment, but Kathryn was deep in thought. 'You're not serious about this man Jake? No, you can't be, because you love my son.'

Kathryn raised her eyes. 'You seem very sure.'

'Woman's intuition.' She smiled. 'The thing you mentioned just now.'

136

Kathryn had to smile; this was a different side of her mother-in-law, and it was even more attractive than that which was familiar. 'I'm not serious about Jake, as you say,' she conceded. 'It's just that I felt I had to have a diversion, and my meetings with him provided it. But I've been worried because he's getting to like me too much,' Kathryn went on to confide. 'I was thinking only a short while ago that it must end.'

'Then end it at once, my dear,' advised her mother-in-law. 'For if Leon should get to know about it, then, believe me, you'd be in for trouble.'

'I'll tell him when I meet him for lunch tomorrow,' promised Kathryn.

But Mrs. Coletis interrupted with, 'Must you keep the date, Kathryn? Can't you phone him?'

'I could, but it wouldn't be very fair.' She looked at her mother-in-law apologetically. 'I shall feel much better if I keep the date and tell him then that it is finished.'

The older woman shrugged resignedly but was plainly disappointed, and she changed the subject to say that Kathryn must have noticed that Marina was more depressed than ever. 'I don't know where it is all going to end,' she added, a quiver in her rich Greek voice. 'Christos has been told what happened and is very depressed, too.'

'Surely there is someone, somewhere, who can diagnose what is wrong?'

'Marina has had all that money can buy in the way of doctors, Kathryn. They are all baffled—oh, one said it was due to some kind of deficiency in the blood, while another said it must be a totally new disease and we would be lucky if a cure came in time for Marina to be saved.'

Kathryn stared. 'You mean . . . they've no hope? I m-mean, did the doctors say she would . . . would die?'

'Of course. Surely Leon mentioned this to you?'

Kathryn shook her head. 'No, he didn't.' She was recalling that moment when the doctor stopped speaking, and she knew the reason was that Leon had given him a warning glance. So Leon did not want her to know that there had been no hope for his sister. Why? After a moment's thought, Kathryn felt she knew the answer: Leon himself did not accept it. He had felt all along that Marina had brought it all on herself after learning of the curse. Kathryn realised that this also answered another question, the one which had troubled her when Leon had said there was much she did not know.

But he had spoken as if there were *several* things she did not know. . . .

'It's strange that Leon didn't tell you that the doctors had given us no hope for Marina,' Mrs. Coletis said, but before either she or Kathryn could speak again, a maid came out to say that Mrs. Coletis was wanted on the telephone. Kathryn was free to continue her stroll, her mind now full of what they had said about her trying to make Leon fall in love with her. The idea had taken root, but although she felt vaguely excited and optimistic, Kathryn dared not at this stage allow a picture of success to enter her mind.

Chapter Eight

It had been a sad parting, but Kathryn had resisted all Jake's entreaties, admitting frankly that as she was still in love with her husband, the idea of this affair had become troublesome to her.

'Well, if ever you should change your mind, or feel you need a friend, you know the number where you can contact me,' he had said at last when, having become resigned, he had asked Kathryn to stay awhile at the hotel where they had had lunch. They had sat in the lounge drinking coffee until, at half-past three, Kathryn had decided she must leave.

Sad though it was, Kathryn felt lighter and freer because of her decision. And she was looking forward to making approaches to her husband, subtle and timid at first, perhaps, but she would let him see that she was ready to forgive him and try to make something of their marriage.

But she reckoned without fate. Leon had seen her with Jake as they came from the hotel and got into his car, for she had agreed to let him drive her home again. As they got in, Jake had kissed her lightly on the lips—a friendly, impulsive gesture which she could not possibly resent. Leon had hurried towards the car, but it had driven off before he reached it—before either occupant had even noticed his approach, in fact. And the first Kathryn knew was when, after she had been home less than five minutes, her husband strode into the salon where she was standing by the open window looking out over the lovely grounds of the villa. On hearing the door open, she spun around, a smile coming instantly to her lips. It froze as she noticed his expression, the lowering brow, the taut features, the compression of the mouth.

'What . . . what . . . ?'

'So you go into town to look at the shops, do you?' he rasped, crossing the room in three or four long strides. 'Liar! You've been meeting another man! I saw you outside the hotel!'

'Just a minute . . .' She faltered, her nerves rioting as fear mounted within her, for never had she expected to see her husband in such a towering rage as this. He terrified her with his aggressive manner—that awful glitter in those harsh serpentine eyes, that satanic expression made more pronounced by the pulsing of a nerve at the side of his mouth. 'It's all over. I . . . I t-told him today—'

'And that was why he was kissing you, I suppose?'

'It was . . . a g-good-bye kiss . . . yes—' She cried out as, with another tiger-like leap, he came close and she felt her wrist taken in a merciless grip. And it seemed as if he had completely lost control, because he brought her to him and shook her until, weak and crying, she begged him to let her go. She swayed, and he caught her again, preventing her from falling. Her face was drained of colour, even her lips were bloodless. Never had she been so afraid, for she felt that the wild beating of her heart must surely bring about a collapse. She put a hand to it, a hand that trembled, and she saw him frown slightly at the action.

'How long have you been having an affair with him?' he demanded grittingly. 'How long, I say!'

'It wasn't an affair,' she quavered, stepping back to put some distance between them. 'We met and had lunch, or . . . or afternoon t-tea, and nothing else happened between us—'

'Except kissing!' he thundered, and it did seem for one terrifying moment that he would do her some serious injury. 'You'd deny all else, I suppose?'

'There isn't anything to deny.'

He looked her over with scornful eyes, his anger appearing to have abated a little. 'No wonder you didn't want your husband! You'd someone else ready to make love to you—'

'Jake has never made love to me—oh, will you listen!' she shouted fiercely. 'It was a friendship and nothing else! It's your evil mind . . .' Her voice trailed off and came to a stop as her throat constricted at his vicious glance.

'Be very careful,' he warned, and now his voice had

taken on a dramatic quietness, the quietness of danger. 'You still haven't seen the worst of me.'

Heaven help me then, if ever I do, she gasped inwardly. Aloud she said, a quiver in her voice, 'You must believe me, Leon. It's important.' She thought miserably of her resolve to follow her mother-in-law's advice and try to make her husband love her. Instead, fate had created a rift that could become far wider and deeper than anything that had gone before. 'There was nothing dishonourable in the relationship between Jake and me.' She was pleading, but he was too inflamed to notice, and she sagged, defeated and wanting only to escape to her room and weep into her pillow. 'You don't believe me, do you?' she added in a strained little voice. 'You *want* to believe the worst of me.'

'What do you expect me to believe?'

She shook her head dumbly. What was the use of trying to convince him? He was too angry, with those eyes kindling with fire and that evil, satanic twist to his mouth. Crimson threads curled up the sides of his mouth, and the blood raced through a vein in his temple.

'Can I go?' she asked in a piteous little voice. 'I've a . . . a headache.'

'When are you supposed to see this man again?' he gritted, ignoring her pathetic little plea.

'I've told you—we've said good-bye.'

He looked at her with icy deliberation. 'I don't believe you,' he said. He appeared to have shed his anger, but his calm and quiet manner seemed even more frightening and she asked again if she could go to her room.

'I can't convince you,' she added, swallowing convulsively to rid her throat of the little ball of misery that had settled there. 'We could be here for hours, arguing . . .' Helplessly she spread her hands. 'I can't convince you,' she said again, and made a tentative move to reach the door. To her surprise, Leon did not attempt to stop her, and she left the room without another word, forgetting to close the door behind her.

It was only when she was in her room that a strange disquiet assailed her and led to the sudden quickening of her heartbeats. Leon, after that first unbridled show of temper, had taken on a very strange manner. Only now did she realise that there was some kind of undercurrent about him, as if he had suddenly conceived an idea. And that was why he had allowed her to leave the room without further questions or demands.

She caught her underlip between her teeth and realised she was hurting herself. But her emotions were rioting; she knew fear without having a reason for that fear. Leon would not do her any real physical harm; his mother and sister were in the house, so she was safe. Yet the image of that satanic countenance intruded into her mind incessantly and she was reminded of his background, the pagan Greeks and the heathen gods they worshipped.

That evening at dinner he was quiet, and yet, when he did speak, there was nothing even remotely antagonistic about him. It was clear to Kathryn that he did not intend to let his mother and sister know that anything was amiss between him and his wife.

Marina was as bright as could be, her chatter happy, her smile appearing often. At this change, Kathryn glanced several times at her husband, to see that he was equally as interested in Marina as she was.

Kathryn stared into the mirror, her big eyes brooding and sad. She had meant everything to be different tonight—oh, she had not actually contemplated a totally uninhibited reunion with her husband, but she had known that if he had tentatively suggested he come to her, she would not have repulsed him. But now . . . she was alone, as she had been alone since making the decision that she and Leon would no longer live normally as man and wife. Alone. . . . She had taken a shower, had lavishly sprayed her sun-gilded body with talc and had slipped into the new diaphanous nightgown she had bought in Athens a few days ago. Her hair shone under the brushing she was giving it. She must have a little cut off, she mused, noticing how long it was getting, and she recalled having heard somewhere that hair and nails grew much faster in a warm climate. It seemed to be true. . . .

Her thoughts stopped, but she continued to stare into the mirror, her heart beginning to thud against her rib cage. Her lips felt stiff as the words left them, spoken in low and husky accents. 'Leon—wh-what do you want?' She hated the expression on his face; it frightened her with its austerity, its hard aspect of ruthlessness and hostility. 'It's . . . it's late. . . .'

A sneer caught his underlip as he used his foot to close the door between his room and hers. Kathryn clasped the hairbrush to her breast, an unconscious gesture which seemed to amuse her husband a little. She saw that he had nothing on beneath his blue-and-gold dressing-gown, which was held together at the front somewhat precariously because the silken cord had not been knotted, one end merely slipped over the other, and it was already beginning to move. He seemed unconscious of it, while she stared in a sort of torpid fascination, seeing in her imagination what must shortly be revealed.

'Late?' with a lift of one eyebrow which seemed to accentuate the satanic lines of his face. He advanced towards her, slowly and with a sort of predatory silence which could have been designed to increase her fear. 'Not too late for what I have come for, my dear.' He pointed to a spot on the carpet and added, in a dangerously soft voice, 'Come here, Kathryn—immediately.'

It was the last words which, strangely, brought the angry colour to her cheeks and the fiery glints to her eyes. 'Don't stand there giving me orders!' she flashed. 'And kindly go back to your own room! You are well aware of the terms to which you have to adhere!' So proper. Pedantic. But she wanted to sound arrogant so that he would take notice of her request, and leave. Inwardly, though, every nerve-cell in her body was quivering, and fear encompassed her heart and mind, for the look on her husband's face was one of sheer primordial mastery and she knew he had come here to take her by force—in anger and for revenge for what he considered a slight, a blow to his arrogant male ego.

She had been out with another man, and she would pay dearly. Yes, she could imagine what had been simmering in his mind earlier when he had allowed her to go, and the same intention had been gradually boiling up during dinner, when he had seemed almost friendly towards her. What kind of evil complexity made up his character? Once again she realised just how little she knew him, this dark forbidding man whom she had married in haste, and in blissful ignorance of what she was in for.

She heard him say, in that soft and threatening tone, 'I told you to come here, and if you know what's good for you, you'll obey me.'

She swallowed convulsively, brushing a hand through her hair and hoping her inner strain was not revealed on the surface. She could not have obeyed him even had she wished to, for the simple reason that fear kept her rooted to the spot where she stood. She saw his eyes narrow as an accompaniment to the swift compression of his mouth. The brush dropped from her nerveless fingers as he leapt across the intervening space. Before she could even guess at his intention, she was jerked against his granite-hard body and her lips brutally possessed, captured and violated as his mastery asserted itself and her struggles crushed almost before they had even begun.

But she did manage to twist her face about after escaping from the pagan cruelty of his mouth, and for a space he let her play with him. It was only when she encountered his glance of mocking humour that she desisted, hot, embarrassed colour sweeping into her face. He took it, holding her chin with slender brown fingers that were like steel rope from which there was no escape. She was in a most humiliating position, her body held with one hawser-strong arm and her face forced up so that her neck hurt as he compelled her to look into his eyes.

Why was he so strong? Why couldn't she fight him? Her love turned to hate in this moment when, with his power and strength, he deliberately humiliated her, showed her who was master. She could not move as his mouth, sensuous and moist, came down on hers; she tried to resist the temptation as he moved his lips in dominant exploration, forcing her lips apart to enable his tongue to explore the dark depths of her mouth. But as the roughness of his tongue slid tantalisingly over the tip of hers, she reluctantly found herself obeying his unspoken command to respond. And when, presently, he drew away, she heard his low, triumphant laugh, felt his hand stray to her breast, felt too the cord of his gown slip. And when next he brought her close, there was nothing between his flesh and hers except the almost negligible presence of the fine nylon of her nightdress.

'Please, Leon—not in anger. . . .' Her lips were quivering and bruised, her eyes filmed with unshed tears. 'If you would only believe me—' She was not allowed to have her say. It was suppressed by the recapture of her mouth, and now it seemed that every vestige of restraint fled and he was the primitive lover and conqueror. She winced at the capture of her breast, gave a protesting little moan as the tender place was hardened to desire within the arrogant pressure of those lean brown fingers. She was craving for fulfilment by the time he stood away, his hands coming to her shoulders to slide the straps of her nightdress down to her waist, and lower. His hands were warm and strong, gliding the length of her body beneath the garment he was removing. His own gown was discarded, and then his muscled arms encircled her and she was compelled against him, intimately close, her breasts flattened against the iron hardness of his chest, her stomach pressed against the coiled-spring strength of his loins. She quivered ecstatically when he spread a hand across her lower back to force her even closer so their naked frames melded and she experienced the exciting male dominance of his manhood. He swung her off her feet, but now she made a show of protest, for she still felt he was taking her by force. But his words of triumphant humour stemmed what she was saying and made her admit to her own willing surrender.

'Don't be a hypocrite, Kathryn. You need me at this moment, need me desperately, so your pretence merely arouses my contempt.' He carried her across the room, walking slowly, his hands hard and possessive, the wiry hair on his chest a stimulant to the erotic nerves in her breasts. Almost roughly, he put her down, his roving hands creating a shock of pure rapture as in their knowledge and experience, they found and caressed and tempted every vulnerable place with the kind of tactile finesse that proved him the perfect lover. She shuddered and arched, desire flaming through her eager body as his hands stroked and then closed, and stroked again before, just at the right moment, he crushed her body beneath the weight of his own.

She clung to him in ecstasy, her throbbing breath an outlet for the wild, tumultuous explosions that were tearing at her nerves and organs and robbing her mind of thought. This was heaven, and all else was vague, without form or reality. She heard her husband's ragged breathing against her ear, heard too the little gasps of ecstasy that escaped the control he put on his voice, resisting as she had done the impulse to cry aloud as the gates of paradise were opened up to him.

Chapter Nine

She awoke to the sun slanting through the space in the drapes where they had not quite met. She rose on one elbow, looking at Leon's dark head on the pillow as memory flooded in.

He had been gentle after all, and as sleep claimed him, he had whispered, so softly that she felt it must not have been intended for her ears at all, 'Good night, dear, and sleep well.'

She had lain awake thinking about it, and into her mind had repeatedly come his assertion that she did not know everything. Why should that particular memory intrude? And why should it seem in some way allied to those whispered words, spoken almost tenderly?

There seemed to be no feasible explanation and, at last, she had dismissed the matter from her mind and fallen into a peaceful, dreamless sleep.

Leon stirred beside her and turned; she saw his eyes harden, and a sudden dejection spread over her.

'What time is it?' he asked abruptly, and when she told him, he slid from the bed, grabbing the dressing-gown from the chair where he had put it last night. She watched him slip it on and tie the cord, and then without so much as another word or even a backward glance, he strode towards the door and passed through it into his room.

She got up immediately, bathed and dressed and met Leon again in the breakfast-room. He looked immaculate as usual, and devastatingly handsome.

'Good morning,' she said, and meant it to sound sarcastic.

He looked hard at her and she sensed an impotent anger which at first she could not understand. 'Good morning,' he responded, and held out her chair for her. She took possession of it and watched him sit down opposite her. They always breakfasted alone; Mrs. Coletis and Marina usually had theirs either in Marina's sitting-room or her mother's. 'I hope you slept well.' Leon's eyes registered sardonic amusement meant to make her blush, but she lifted her chin instead.

'Very well, thank you.' She reached over to take a piece of toast.

Leon said tersely, 'I take it that you fully understand that this affair with Jake is finished?'

'I've already told you it is.'

'And I said I don't believe you,' he said, and rebellion was instantly born within her. She'd let him believe what he liked!

Her eyes glinted as temper flared. She forgot the

tender resolution she had made, the half-promise given to her mother-in-law. Leon was trying her patience, and she retaliated instinctively. 'I believe I told you that my life is my own.'

'Not while you are my wife.' Although his voice was quiet enough, a wrathful flood of crimson stained his cheeks and his nostrils thinned unpleasantly. How pagan he looked! How domineering and superior! Could she expect to win a battle with such a man? Nevertheless, she had to try, for it was not in her nature to be subjugated, treated as if she were one of his Greek countrywomen, used to submitting to the masculine dominance which prevailed in their country.

'You married me under false pretences and, therefore, I do not consider myself obligated in any way to obey your wishes, much less your orders,' she added with a flash of defiance which instantly brought more angry blood to his face.

He looked directly at her across the table, his eyes lynx-like beneath those straight black brows. 'In Greece the husband is the master, and you are in Greece, married to a Greek. I shall not allow you to continue to defy me.' Still quiet the voice, but determined and expressive.

Kathryn, unable to find an immediate retort, helped herself to fruit from the bowl of mangoes and bananas. But her hand trembled and her heart was sad, so sad that tears came unbidden to her eyes. She blinked rapidly to prevent them from falling onto her cheeks, for surely that would give away her secret—that this rift was far more painful to her than to him. But perhaps he knew it already, she mused after a time. He knew she had once been in love with him, and although she felt she had convinced him that she no longer had any feelings for him, he was so astute that her responses of last night might have told him far more than she would have wished. A deeper sadness filled her heart as the memory of that came back to her with profound emotion and intensity. So loving they had been with each other. . . .

'Just what made you enter into an affair with this man?' Leon broke the silence, and she glanced up from cutting herself a piece of mango.

'Does it matter?' she returned in a tone more flat than she would have wished.

'Be careful,' warned her husband dangerously. 'You've seen something of my temper, but not the worst of it.'

She coloured and averted her face, angry and humiliated at this reminder of his mastery over her. 'You can't domineer over me,' she said quietly. 'I'm my own mistress, no matter what you say to the contrary. You are the one to blame in all this, but your attitude can hardly be described as one of guilt. You're far too arrogant and—'

'Shall we keep to the point,' he cut in impatiently. 'This affair—it has ended, understand?'

'You mean, I shan't see Jake again?'

'What else?' His face was dark, his manner withdrawn. 'You're not obtuse; you understand what I'm saying.'

'I can leave you,' she challenged. 'And if you try me too far, I shall.'

'Again, I don't believe you.'

'Oh, and why?' She looked at him interestedly, the knife idle in her hands.

'Because you're far too comfortable here, that is one reason. Reason two is that whatever is lacking in our marriage certainly has nothing to do with the physical side. I give you what you need—'

'Shut up!' she flared. 'Let's leave that side out of it!' She was hot and embarrassed and her appetite was gone. She put down the knife and threw her napkin on the table. 'I refuse to carry on this kind of a conversation!' She made to rise, but her husband was there; an arrogant, masterful pressure on her shoulder compelled her to remain where she was. 'Let me go!' she cried, but the pressure increased, painfully so.

'Get your breakfast,' he ordered harshly. 'I assure you that if you don't obey me, I shall force it down your throat.'

She stared and gasped, beginning to shake her head, but one upward glance confirmed the seriousness of his threat, and she picked up her napkin again and spread it across her knees. Leon released her and went back to his chair.

No more was said about Jake—in fact, neither spoke at all, not even when, the meal finished, they left the room, Leon by the door and Kathryn by the French window leading to the patio.

Later the same day Christos came for a brief visit. After seeing Marina, who was reading on the verandah of her room, he sought out Kathryn, and as soon as she saw his expression, she guessed that something of importance was going to be said to her.

154

'I really came especially to talk to you,' he said without preamble when he caught up to her. She was wandering along a shady garden path at the end of which was an ornamental pool where brightly coloured fish swam and where a rocky cascade sparkled in the sun as its crystal-clear waters tumbled in wild abandon into the pool. On the edge of the pool were many different greens and other, brighter colours, for flowers grew in abundance, and the whole area around the pool was a veritable fairyland of colour and perfume, of light and shade and music, and, most of all, tranquillity.

'You did?' Kathryn feigned surprise as she added, looking up into his handsome English features, 'I'm honoured, Christos. Is there something important you have to say to me?'

'It's questions, mostly.'

'Yes?' She sauntered on, and he slowed his steps to match hers.

'There's a seat along there . . . ' He pointed, and she nodded her head. 'Will you sit with me for a while?'

'Of course. That was where I was going, in fact.'

They reached the bench, a little rustic seat for two beneath the shade of a jacaranda tree with a flaring hibiscus hedge around three sides of it. It faced the pool, with the waterfall to the right. A couple of gaily plumaged ducks were gliding over the water where, at the far end, it was smooth and gleaming and bordered with aquatic plants.

'You've noticed that Marina is getting worse?' His voice had changed dramatically; it was now broken and low, and in addition Kathryn could have sworn that there were tears in his eyes. A man crying. Oh, but that

155

was something that caught at her heartstrings! Nothing so sad as to see a man cry.

'We all have,' she answered gently, and although she would have liked to utter words of comfort, they just would not come.

'Kathryn, until this new disaster, when she collapsed after leaving the wheelchair, I felt, like Leon, that Marina's illness was something she had brought on herself, that it was a psychological phenomenon.'

'But you had nothing to support that idea,' she just had to say.

'Did Leon have anything to support his idea?'

He did, thought Kathryn; he knew of the curse, knew just how strongly it had affected his sister.

'I don't know just what you are getting at,' she said guardedly.

'I felt that Marina's illness was some kind of malady brought on by a mental defect—'

'Mental defect?' swiftly and protestingly. 'Marina's mind is perfectly normal, Christos.'

'What is normal? By what do we measure normality? Are you normal? Do you do everything rationally, logically?'

Kathryn frowned. She was acutely aware of her attitude towards Leon that morning at breakfast when, although she had definitely given Jake up, she had then gone out of her way to convince her husband that she had no intention of giving him up.

'You have a point,' she conceded, but went on to say again that Marina was what would generally be termed normal.

'You gave her a ring.' Brief and emphasised the

statement, which was followed by the even more brief, 'Why?'

'Why?' Kathryn played for time without knowing what she wanted time for anyway.

'Yes, why? It's a very valuable ring.'

'I don't think I understand.'

'Oh, yes you do, Kathryn. That ring matched some other jewellery which Marina has.'

'Have you seen this other jewellery?' she inquired with interest, and he nodded his head saying yes, he had seen it, a long time ago, when Marina was well and happy.

'Marina said a strange thing on her birthday. She said she would soon be better, and like a flash she was showing me the ring. "This will make me well, Christos, just you see." She seemed very young, Kathryn, in that particular moment, like a child—a trusting child, yes, trusting and innocent. I loved her dearly before, but at that moment she was like an angel, so innocent, so trusting.'

'Trusting—you have used the word several times—'

'She trusted the ring.' The cool grey eyes were narrowed and searching. 'You know something. You must, or you'd not have given it to her.

Kathryn paused, debating whether to tell him everything—yes, she realised, it would have to be everything or nothing at all, since to tell him part would assuredly whet his appetite for more.

'Did Marina draw your attention to the fact that the ring matched the other jewellery she had?' inquired Kathryn at length, bypassing his query for the time being.

Christos shook his head. 'I rather think she'd forgotten I'd ever seen the other jewellery.'

'She must have known you'd be puzzled by her stating that the ring would make her well?'

'She seemed in a dream—sort of,' explained Christos with a reflective frown. 'Excited and . . . optimistic. Kathryn,' he said urgently, 'I must know what this is all about!'

Kathryn still hesitated, for while she was deeply sympathetic towards Christos, she was at the same time reluctant to explain everything to him, since this must include the circumstances of her marriage, and its failure. But even as she was trying to decide, Christos was speaking again, saying he wanted the mystery explained.

'Mystery?'

'Mystery!' he echoed affirmatively. 'Please don't keep me on tenterhooks, Kathryn,' he begged. 'It's something bordering on the unnatural, isn't it?'

Kathryn was swift to deny this. 'Rather is it psychological,' she went on, having decided to tell him the whole. 'Do you believe in curses?'

'Curses?' He frowned. 'No, certainly not!'

'Nor did I at one time, nor am I sure I do now. But some strange things have happened to people owning that jewellery.' She went on to relate everything since the moment she had dug up the ring in her garden in England. Christos was fascinated, speechlessly so, and could only stare, wide-eyed, until she had finished.

'I can't believe in a curse,' he said slowly after a long and frowning silence. 'It isn't possible that this fellow could put a curse on the jewellery. And if he could,' added Christos inconsistently, 'the curse wouldn't last this long, or affect any family other than the St. Cleres.'

'That's exactly how I saw it,' agreed Kathryn. 'And so I wore the ring, and enjoyed wearing it. But . . . but after what happened about my marriage . . .' She trailed off, half-regretting this particular confidence, yet at the same time telling herself again that it would be impossible to leave part of the story out.

'You must feel devastated. It was wrong of Leon to marry you for that reason, and yet . . .' He broke off and looked apologetically at her. 'From my own, selfish viewpoint, Kathryn, if it had worked I'd only have been able to be glad . . . Oh, but no, I ought not to have been glad!' Distress looked out from his eyes, and Kathryn automatically placed a soothing hand on his arm.

'Don't worry about it, Christos,' she advised in gentle tones. 'It's done anyway, so nothing can undo it. Regrets are futile after something has already come to pass.' Her smile was jaded as she looked at him. 'I only wish there had been some profit in it for someone.' Sadly, she shook her head. 'What is going to happen to Marina now . . .?' Again she stopped, this time to look at him with deep compassion in her lovely eyes. 'And you, Christos? What will you do with your life?'

He shook his head; she saw his lip quiver, and her heart caught. 'I suppose the situation's no different than it was before she became so excited, so sure she would be well after she owned the ring.' He paused a moment, then changed the subject. 'You're a rather wonderful person, Kathryn. I think Leon must be crazy not to have fallen in love with you before now.'

'He has someone else. You know that.'

'Eugenia?'

'You saw him with her in Glifadha, remember? I've just told you I overheard the conversation between Marina and her mother.'

'It was regrettable that you did!' came the expressive comment.

'But best that I know where I stand. It's not my wish to live in a fool's paradise.'

'Where ignorance is bliss . . .' he quoted, but she shook her head.

'The truth would have come out sometime.'

'I don't believe there's anything between Leon and Eugenia now,' he said in an effort to raise her spirits.

'Then why was he with her?'

'It could have been an accidental meeting. It does happen, you know.'

'But when you told Marina you'd seen them together, you must have wondered why they were with one another, for otherwise you'd not have mentioned it at all.'

'I suppose I was curious, at the time,' he admitted reflectively. 'Still, I'd not condemn him out of hand, Kathryn. So much heartache can occur through misjudging people.'

Kathryn brooded on this, recalling vividly her husband's conviction that she had been having an affair with Jake, and his refusal to believe her when she told him it was ended now. That had caused heartache

. . . and she was now causing *herself* heartache by believing the worst of her husband.

'He did say it was all over between him and Eugenia,' she murmured thoughtfully.

'Then it probably is, because Leon wouldn't lie.'

'Perhaps you're right. If it is true that there's no longer anything between them, then there could be a chance for our marriage.'

It was Christos' turn to do the comforting; he touched her hand and then covered it with his palm.

'You're so lovely that he'll not be able to help himself. He'll fall head over heels in love with you!' He paused and smiled at her blushes. 'Are you quite sure he hasn't fallen in love with you already?'

'Quite sure,' she answered, thinking of his brutal treatment of her after he had seen her with Jake. He had refused to listen when she tried to convince him that it was all ended, and she strongly suspected, too, that he did not believe it had all been platonic anyway.

'Why are you so sure, Kathryn?' asked Christos gently.

She smiled faintly and shook her head. 'I cannot tell you how I know, but I do know, Christos.'

He left soon afterwards, and that evening Leon informed her that he would be away for a couple of days. 'I'm going to Rhodes,' he ended tersely. They were in the salon alone, waiting to be joined by Mrs. Coletis and Marina. But Marina had been crying on and off all afternoon, and Kathryn had an idea that the girl would not be joining them at all.

'Rhodes,' she repeated, wishing with all her heart

she could say, 'I am coming with you, darling,' but instead she looked at him with an expressionless gaze and said that one day she would like to see the lovely island.

To that he made no comment, nor did he come to her that night. She was lonely and depressed. She had asked Christos what was going to happen to his life, but now she wondered what was going to happen to hers. She and Leon could not go on for the rest of their lives like this . . . and yet, could she bear to say a final good-bye to him? She closed her eyes tightly, but the tears oozed through her lashes. She buried her face in her pillow and wept unrestrainedly into it.

A few days later she was wandering through the narrow streets of the Plaka when she saw Jake coming towards her and she stopped, her eyes darting about to seek for a place where she could hide until he had passed. But he had seen her and his smile came, a weak attempt, it was true, but it seemed to lighten Kathryn's spirits and she went forward eagerly to meet him.

'Oh, but it's great to see you!' he exclaimed, taking her hand in his. 'What are you doing—just strolling?'

'That's right.'

'It shouldn't be like this.' He sighed as he spoke. 'You, a new bride, walking about aimlessly instead of enjoying these most precious days and months.'

'I don't want to talk about it. . . .' Her voice broke, and to her consternation, she started to cry.

'Let's get away from here!' He was still holding her hand as he guided her towards a narrow alleyway which took them out of the main bustle of the area. 'I know of a tiny *cafeneion* which is frequented only by a few of the locals. It's very quiet at this time of day.'

'I'm all right . . .' She drew a hand across her eyes. 'It was just a recollection . . .'

'Of what, dear?'

She did not speak until they were seated in the shady little café, vines tangled above their heads, the table in front of them covered with a snow-white cloth.

'Leon saw us coming from the hotel. . . .' She went on to tell him how her husband had tried to reach them before they could get into the car but failed. 'He was furious,' she ended, clenching her jaws as tears gathered again in her eyes.

'That was unfortunate, but surely you told him that we'd said a final good-bye?'

'He wouldn't believe me.' She felt disloyal, talking about Leon like this, yet at the same time it was a relief to unburden herself to someone she knew she could trust. However, she soon changed the subject, telling him what had happened to Marina. He watched her intently, and she saw that he was keenly interested in her description of the occurrence.

He was still thoughtful when she had finished, but spoke at last. 'So it's a bone defect? Nothing to do with the curse.'

'Nothing. I don't now believe in the curse.'

'I never did believe in it—oh, don't make any mistakes, it is possible for people to bring on illnesses themselves. But as for the effectiveness of a curse . . .' He spread his hands and shook his head. 'That I cannot accept. However,' he added almost eagerly, 'I've a friend at the hospital, a Dr. Yannis Serapoulos, who has been carrying out extensive reasearch in the field of bone diseases; he specialises in that particular aspect of medicine. He's made some wonderful discoveries and effected cures in cases where other doctors have given up hope.' He stopped and looked questioningly at her. 'Shall I get Yannis to go along and look at her?'

Kathryn's eyes had brightened. 'That would be possible, I'm sure. Oh, Jake, do you think there is any hope?'

'I can't say, obviously, but at least if she saw Yannis it would be doing something, whereas at present there is nothing being done.'

'It's all been done, according to the doctors Marina has seen. In fact, I learned only two days ago that they'd given up hope; they'd told her mother and brother that she was going to die.'

The waiter came along with a tray on which were two glasses of white wine and a *mezé*. Jake paid him.

He looked at the tip and said, *'Efharisto!'* then went away smiling.

'So they'd all given up hope?' Jake shook his head sadly. 'I do hope Yannis can do something for her.'

'Her brother—my husband—did not give up hope. I feel he was determined not to accept the verdict of the doctors.' She went on to mention the plight of Marina's mother, who wanted to get married but would not do so while her daughter was ill and needed looking after. 'Mrs. Coletis would never let anyone else take care of her,' she ended.

'When shall I make the appointment for?' Jake asked

when, three-quarters of an hour later, they said good-bye outside the *cafeneion*.

'Suppose I talk with Leon and then phone you?' she suggested.

'That'll be fine.' He paused a moment in thought. 'The fact that Marina walked those few paces will, I am sure, be of great interest to Yannis. It was most strange, don't you think?'

'I feel that Marina could have convinced herself that, having got possession of the ring, she could walk.'

Jake's eyes widened and he nodded slowly. 'We get back to the psychological aspect, don't we?'

'Yes. Mind you, it's only my idea, and it could be wrong. But she was so excited when I gave her the ring and she said to Christos that the ring would make her better.'

'I must mention all this to Yannis, as the more he knows of the case, the better. He'll be able to ponder on it before he ever sees the patient.' Suddenly he frowned. 'But what about Marina's initial depression and brooding, the introversion which you've mentioned?' His frown cleared. 'Of course!' he exclaimed. 'She *thought* it was cursed and so became afraid, and that led automatically to her imagining she was becoming ill—which of course she was. But the loss of the use of her legs was a *real* illness—'

'Which came almost immediately upon her so-called imaginary illness! What a coincidence, Jake.'

'Certainly a coincidence.' He nodded, pursing his lips. 'Well, we shall have to see what my friend makes of it all.' He looked at her and his eyes became dark. 'This really is good-bye, isn't it?' he said.

'Yes, Jake. Thank you for some very happy hours.'

Suddenly he kissed her and was gone; she watched until he had turned the corner, and then walked slowly in the same direction.

She did not know what to expect when, after telling Leon of the meeting with Jake and the suggestion he had made, she waited, a little breathlessly, for his reaction. His face had at first taken on a dark expression, helped by the blood easing up along the sides of his mouth; his eyes, too, had narrowed and smouldered, and Kathryn had hurried on, desperate to overshadow the actual meeting with the fact that Jake might be able to help Marina, through his friend Yannis Serapoulos, the bone specialist.

'So you had ended the affair, you said,' began Leon, then stopped, and his features relaxed. He seemed faintly ashamed of what he had intended to say to her, yet relieved that he had held his anger in check. She sagged with relief, and a long breath issued from her lips. She was pale, but the main thought occupying her mind was in fact the possibility of a cure for her sister-in-law. Leon, too, was occupied on the same lines, and so, mused Kathryn, they were united instead of aggressive towards one another.

'The affair—as you call it—is ended, Leon.' Kathryn broke the silence, her voice earnest, her eyes frank and wide. 'Today's meeting was sheer accident, but if it leads to help for Marina, then it was meant to be . . . fate.' She looked at him with a touching glance, her eyes moist and dark. 'It might mean she has to go into hospital—'

'That won't matter.' Leon's voice was soft, almost gentle, and her heart caught. 'This specialist has cured patients whose cases have been hopeless, you said?'

She nodded and repeated everything that Jake had said, although she had told Leon most of it already.

'Jake says this Dr. Serapoulos has recently made some outstanding discoveries during his extensive research.'

Leon's face became tense. 'If we should raise Marina's hopes—and mother's—and then nothing came of it . . .'

'I've already thought of that, Leon,' answered Kathryn seriously. 'But if we don't try, then she's going to die. . . . Yes, I know that the doctors attending her have told you there's no hope,' she went on quickly, seeing his start of surprise. 'Why didn't you tell me?' she asked curiously.

'Because I didn't believe it!' he stated vehemently. 'Marina's young; why should anyone give up hope?'

'I thought that was the reason,' she said. 'I can understand your reluctance to accept a verdict like that, but, on the other hand, what would eventually have happened to her?'

Leon stared at her curiously. 'You talk as if you are sure she will be cured,' he said, and it was her turn to stare.

'Yes,' she murmured in a faraway tone. 'Yes, I did . . . and I believe she will be.'

Dr. Serapoulos came the following afternoon and was with Marina for over two hours. When he came away, he asked Leon if she could go into hospital for observation.

'You believe there is hope?' Kathryn, watching her husband as he spoke, thought she had never seen anyone look so grey and anxious. His face was drawn, his mouth tight, as if he was clenching his teeth together.

'I cannot give you any real hope at this stage,' answered the doctor guardedly, 'but I'd like to have her under observation. Her case is a challenge; I cannot say I have ever had a case quite like hers, but recently a new bone disease has been brought to light, a disease found only in remote jungles. I feel this disease is the one which could be affecting your sister, but I certainly would not hazard any kind of guess until I have had her in the hospital for at least a week.'

Leon said, after a pause, 'I believe you have been told about the so-called curse?'

The doctor nodded his head. 'Jake told me the whole story. Of course, there was no curse. Unfortunately, though, these stories do affect some people, and your sister, having heard of the misfortunes which had befallen previous owners of the jewellery, brooded and worried until she became ill, all owing to allowing her imagination to run riot. Then this happened to her legs and both she and you quite naturally concluded that both symptoms were related, when, in fact, they weren't.' He paused, and for a moment Kathryn examined his features. Full-faced and dark-skinned, he had the appearance of the typical Greek, but with a very high forehead and eyes that seemed to be grey rather than the usual brown. He was stockily built, immaculately dressed, and his black hair shone with cleanliness. 'Marina would have had the bone disease even if she had never seen the jewellery.' He looked at Leon and asked again if his sister could enter the hospital in Athens.

'Of course, if she is agreeable,' replied Leon. 'I suppose we can visit her quite often?'

'Certainly,' with a slight inclination of his head. 'While she is under observation, you can visit her anytime you wish. She will be in a private ward and given every comfort,' the doctor went on to assure him. 'She has a mother, Jake was saying.'

'Yes, but Mother had to go out this afternoon. It was a previous arrangement and I assured her that she need not cancel it.'

'Her mother will need to give her consent to Marina's entering hospital.'

'She will certainly be glad to do so,' Leon assured him at once. 'When do you want my sister to go in?'

'As soon as possible—tomorrow morning, I would say.'

'It shall be done.'

'Would you like an ambulance?'

'I'd prefer to bring her in the car. She's very highly strung at the present time, owing to what happened when she tried to walk, so I think we'll dispense with the ambulance.'

'You are wise. We want to keep her as calm as possible.' He looked at Kathryn, made a stiff little bow and indicated his intention of leaving.

Leon showed him out, and when he came back he said quietly, unemotionally, 'Thank you, Kathryn.'

'We don't know yet what is going to happen.' She had coloured at his gently spoken words and her heart felt full. 'Don't thank me yet, Leon, in case we all are disappointed.'

'Somehow, I do not feel we shall be.'

Chapter Ten

The next week was an anxious one for everyone at the villa, as even the servants were caught up in the drama of the situation. Christos was a regular visitor at the hospital, as were Kathryn and her husband and, of course, Mrs. Coletis and Demetrius.

Demetrius spoke to Kathryn, asking if it were she who had been responsible for Marina's being in the care of Dr. Serapoulos.

'It was really through Jake, a friend of mine who is a student at the hospital,' she returned.

He looked at her with an odd expression as he said, 'Leon's mother mentioned him a couple of weeks ago. She said you had finished with him.' Demetrius' voice was accented and rather gruff, his expression faintly anxious. 'Don't let anything come between you and your husband, my dear,' he said, and patted her hand in a fatherly sort of way.

She smiled and said convincingly that she would not be seeing Jake again. 'At least,' she amended, 'not by pre-arrangement.'

'Well, that is wise of you.' His eyes flicked over her lovely face. 'Don't you worry about a thing, Kathryn. Be an optimist like me, and tell yourself that all will come right in the end.'

'I might just do that,' she promised, and suddenly her heart felt light.

At the end of a week Dr. Serapoulos told Leon and his mother that he would now begin treatment, but warned them not to expect any swift, dramatic change.

'But you have hope of a cure?' from Leon with unfamiliar intensity.

'I certainly have hope or I'd not be giving your sister treatment.'

Marina herself seemed lethargic, as if she had no faith in the doctor's ability to help her. Kathryn tried to shake her out of her torpor, but without success. Christos, however, had more success, for he was very firm—stern at times—as he told Marina she had best get better because he planned to be married to her before another year was past.

Kathryn was there when Marina said, her lovely black hair contrasting starkly with the gleaming whiteness of the pillow, 'You still love me, then?'

'You know I do. I have never loved anyone else, and I never shall.'

'But what about—?'

'It was always you, darling. Don't let me down. Promise you'll fight hard for my sake?'

At that point Kathryn rose from her chair and, after bending to kiss her sister-in-law's forehead, left them together.

The treatment had been progressing for about ten days when Dr. Serapoulos stated quite firmly that there had been an improvement in Marina's condition. And after another week he said she would walk again.

'You're sure?' It was Mrs. Coletis who spoke, and there was a distinct tremor in her voice.

'I never raise anyone's hopes unless I am sure I won't have to disappoint them.'

'It seems too good to be true,' breathed Kathryn when they were all at home. Demetrius had decided to come back with them and stay for dinner—if they would have him, dressed as he was.

'It's a miracle,' declared Mrs. Coletis. She turned to her daughter-in-law. 'And it is all due to you, dear. It is you we have to thank.'

Kathryn coloured delicately and glanced in her husband's direction. This business of Marina's going into hospital, the tension and anxiety, the raised hopes and then the intrusion of doubts—all these had served to bring the family close . . . and especially did Kathryn sense a change in her husband's feelings towards her. He was never harsh or even cool. It never struck her at this time that the change in him could be the result of changes in *her* manner towards *him*. In this situation, which so deeply affected them all, Kathryn had forgotten wrongs done to her. They would have seemed negligible anyway in face of this crisis, for they all had been aware that, had the doctor's verdict been that he could not help Marina, they'd have known she would die, perhaps a slow lingering death. She continued to look at Leon; their eyes seemed to hold and neither wished to look away. A slow and difficult smile rose to Kathryn's lips; it was a moment filled with tension, a moment she felt she would remember for the rest of her life.

Leon broke the silence at last, adding his thanks to those of his mother. Demetrius' whole attention was held, and so was that of Mrs. Coletis. The older woman's eyes were bright, evidence of tears unshed. Kathryn knew she would never shed them here, for she possessed that kind of enviable control which insured her against breaking down in public. If she had to weep, thought Kathryn, it would be in the quiet and privacy of her own room.

It was much later that Kathryn said to her husband, 'Do you intend to get rid of that jewellery?' And when he made no immediate reply, she added on a note of urgency, 'I think you should, Leon.' They were on the verandah of her bedroom, both clad in dressing-gowns. Kathryn had been there alone for twenty minutes or so before Leon joined her. She had not expected him and she had turned with a ready smile . . . and an invitation. He had come to stand beside her, cool and fresh from the shower, his wet hair glistening in the moon's argent glow which brought out the strands of grey and painted them bright silver. He had used a subtly perfumed body lotion which made her think of mountains and heather and that nostalgic tang of the sea, all mingled together to stir her senses and draw her a little closer to where he stood. The air around them was balmy, the breeze fresh, lifting the hair from Kathryn's forehead, colouring her pale cheeks.

'Why should we let it go?' he asked with a slight smile. 'We know now that there is nothing sinister about it.'

Her gaze was pensive; she was recalling that moment when she had come upon the ring and had nearly tossed it away.

'I don't think I want to see Marina wearing it,' she said, and at the hint of apology in her voice she felt her hand covered, gently, as it rested on the rail.

'I very much doubt that she will wear it,' he returned.

'Then why keep it?'

He said nothing for a moment, and the silence between them became heavy. 'You perhaps feel you ought to have the ring back?' was his unexpected query, and she instantly shook her head.

'The pieces must be kept together—'

'You are thinking of the curse,' he broke in, and now she detected the merest hint of amusement in his tone. 'But, as I've just reminded you, there is no curse.'

A difficult laugh escaped her and she turned her face to his. 'I'd forgotten already, Leon. Do you suppose, though, that any of us really could forget? If Marina wore any of it, we should all be uncomfortable because memories must inevitably crowd in on us.'

'But I have just said I doubt very much that she will wear it.'

'Then why keep it?' she said, repeating the question she had already asked.

'The decision lies with Marina. We shall have to see how she feels about selling it. Father bought it for her, and she might feel sentimental about it.'

Kathryn shook her head. 'It has caused too much heartache, Leon.' A plea in her voice, which was husky and faintly sad, for she was now thinking about her own situation, and the marriage which had come about solely because of that ring. 'Marina has suffered and . . . and so have I . . . well, both you and I have suffered . . .' She looked at him, saw the tenseness of his jaw as if he were suddenly suppressing anger.

'You said you didn't love me. Does that mean that you care for someone else . . . Jake?'

She turned away abruptly, more owing to his unexpected change of subject than anything else. She did not for one moment realise that her action could be misconstrued. 'Let's leave Jake out of it,' she began.

He interrupted her to say curtly, 'I'm afraid we can't leave Jake out of it!'

'I've told you, several times, that there is nothing between Jake and me. We've said good-bye, and that's the end of the affair.'

'So you now admit it was an affair?' Grim the tone, but with an undercurrent which was unfathomable.

'No, I do not admit it was an affair!'

'Then why did you refer to it as that just now?'

'A figure of speech, for want of a better description of the perfectly innocent friendship which sprang up between Jake and me as a result of my loneliness and . . . and despair.' She paused to clear the hurtful blockage in her throat. 'My marriage had collapsed after only a few weeks. I needed comfort, and Jake just happened along. I tripped and he caught me, saving me from falling. He sensed that I was unhappy and invited me to have afternoon tea with him . . .' She broke off and spread her hands. 'It's all in the past, so why should I talk about it?' A shuddering sigh followed her words, and she felt the fingers of Leon's hand tighten over hers. She wanted to cry for what she had lost, and yet, paradoxically, she knew that deep in her heart she was praying that all was *not* lost, that she could make Leon love her. She had thought a great deal lately about children, feeling that if they had a child, then surely Leon would love the mother.

And she rather suspected she was already carrying Leon's child. . . .

'So you don't love Jake,' mused Leon at last. 'Do you love me, Kathryn?' Leon's voice had lowered; it was edged with tenderness, and she accepted that he was filled with gratitude towards her for what she had done for his sister—the help which, after all, had come in a very different way than had originally been planned. She looked at him, and could not give him a truthful answer because, since he did not love her, an admission of her own love would be far too humiliating.

It did not occur to Kathryn that he had some special reason for the question, and so she said, slowly, as if reluctant to voice something which, though a lie, was very necessary, 'No, I c-can't love you—not when I know you married me under false pretences. . . .' She brought her voice to a trailing stop. If she were to make her husband love her, she must not keep reminding him of what he had done to her. Again the tears came close; she did not know they glistened in her eyes, or of the effect they had on her husband. She did not know that she seemed especially attractive to him tonight, that he was finding a tender translucency in the pallor of her face, the alabaster quality of her skin, or that the moonglow flattered her in a way which Leon found irresistible. Her over-gown had come loose and her low-cut nightdress revealed breasts that had filled a little lately, honey-tan curves alluring to her husband's appreciative eyes. She saw a muscle twist and throb in his throat, saw his eyes shaded by lashes deliberately lowered to hide his expression.

'You loved me when you married me.' His voice was flat, a betrayal that he believed her when she said she did not love him now.

'I did, very deeply.'

'So deeply that it has died already.' Dry and sardonic the tone now; she hated him in this kind of mood. He always seemed so superior, high above her like a god on an unreachable pedestal.

'There are some things that even deep love cannot weather.'

His gaze was morose. 'Are you telling me there's no future for us, Kathryn?'

She was startled, frightened. Perhaps she had carried her injured feelings too far; perhaps Leon had had enough of tensions and strained relations, of her coldness and her pride. Yes, she was afraid, and the quiver

in her voice was a betrayal of this fear. 'You mean
. . . are you suggesting we . . . we h-have a separation?' The child—if there was to be one . . . Kathryn
had never contemplated having a one-parent child. It
wasn't as if she had anyone to go to, a mother or even
an aunt; she had no one who would want her with a
child.

Leon scanned her pallid face and his eyes narrowed a
little. 'You are not keen on the idea?' His voice was
grim and curt; he was adopting a superior manner, and
she felt it was done deliberately to increase her fear.
'You don't like the thought of resuming the life you
were living before your marriage?'

She could not answer for a while. It was unthinkable
that she should admit to loving him, and yet, if he really
was suggesting a divorce, then she would have to lower
her pride and tell him she wanted to stay. And if she did
that, he must quite logically guess that she still loved
him.

'Well?' he prompted in a very soft voice. He had
removed his hand; she felt the cool air on hers, and an
unaccountable shiver quickened her whole body.

'I . . . it . . . it has to b-be your decision . . .' She
faltered, blinking rapidly to stem the tears which threatened to fall. 'I suppose . . . suppose that Eugenia . . .'
What on earth had she meant to say?

'Could it be that you are jealous of Eugenia?' he
questioned in a dry voice. 'I must say, you've been
interested in her from time to time.'

'You were in love with her—probably still are.'

'No,' he denied, still in that same dry tone, 'I am not

179

in love with her and haven't been for some time. In fact,' he went on thoughtfully, 'I rather think I was never in love with her.'

'Never?' She blinked at him, nerves suddenly quivering.

'There was something,' he admitted reflectively. 'Something strong.'

'Is that a question?' Faint amusement in his manner now . . . and perception in his eyes.

'It doesn't matter,' she returned flatly, and she brushed a hand across her face, very much in the manner of a child who, bewildered and tired, is reluctantly feeling ready to go to sleep.

The action seemed to move Leon deeply, but his voice had not softened in any appreciable way as he said, 'So you do not want a separation?'

She looked at him through shadowed eyes. 'I've said, it's your decision.'

Leon moved a little closer; she could feel the hardness of his thigh against her. 'Kathryn,' he said, and now his voice was infinitely gentle, 'I feel it is time we both lowered our pride. I've stubbornly held on to mine, believing you were telling the truth when you stated that your love for me was dead. I, like you, dear, could not bring myself to confess to loving someone who did not love me. But you do love me, very dearly, and I love you. So you see, darling, it is high time we acted like sensible people and stopped running around in circles.' He would have pulled her into his arms, but she stepped away, to stand there staring at him as if she could not believe her ears.

'You love me?' Her voice was sceptical. 'When . . . ?
No, this is gratitude and you're just saying you love me
so that I won't be too unhappy, so I won't insist on
leaving you!'

'Darling,' said Leon, trying to be patient, 'don't
begin all over again. Gratitude? Yes, certainly I am
grateful for what you've done for Marina, but I love
you as well.'

She shook her head, saying reluctantly, 'It's gratitude . . . it *must* be—'

'Let me show you whether it's love or not,' he
begged, still having trouble with his patience. 'Let me
take you to bed—'

'*That* wouldn't prove anything, and you know it! It's
just . . . just lust!'

'My heavens, Kathryn, you are asking for it!' No
restraint on his temper now as he gripped her by the
shoulders and shook her thoroughly. 'A more perverse
woman I have never met! I love you! *Love you!* Does
that convince you?'

She began to cry, the result of overwrought nerves,
she decided. These past two weeks had obviously taken
their toll. 'I don't believe . . . I mean,' she added
hastily, when it seemed he would shake her again, 'you
didn't love me when you married me.'

'What the devil does that signify?' he demanded
wrathfully.

'It was a dastardly trick.'

He looked at her warningly, holding her at arm's
length. 'Kathryn,' he said in a dangerously soft voice,
'do you know how very close you are at this moment to

the beating of your life?' She coloured vividly and tried to pull away, but in vain. 'Yes, my girl,' grimly and with another little shake, 'you are about to be thrown across my knee—'

'No!' She began to struggle in earnest. 'Touch me and I shall scream for help!'

'No you won't,' he said with a hint of amused mockery. 'Your pride won't let you.'

So right! Yet she was not going to submit to the spanking he had threatened her with.

'Let me go,' she cried, still struggling even though she admitted there was no chance of success. Leon's muscled hands, curving sinuously around her shoulders —and leaving bruises, she was sure—were far too strong for her puny attempts at escape.

'Say you love me!' he commanded.

'If . . . if I thought you were speaking the truth when you say you love me—' she began, but he interrupted her before she could finish.

'Say you love me,' he ordered again, 'because if you don't, Kathryn, then it's the spanking. The choice is yours.'

Her colour heightened, but still she hesitated, uneasily aware of doubts still lingering in her mind. If it was merely gratitude he felt for her . . . 'Well,' came her husband's voice decisively as he pulled a chair towards him, 'it looks as if it's the beating.'

'You wouldn't dare!'

'No? We shall soon know, shan't we?'

She lifted her hands to push them against his chest. 'If only I could believe you,' she said as she gave a push which surprised them both. She was free, having taken him unaware like that, and she fled into her bedroom. But he was there almost at once and pulled her into his arms. His mouth, hard and possessive, crushed hers in a kiss that left her gasping for breath.

'Leon . . . I—' Her mouth was claimed again, even before she could gulp the air she needed. He was pushing the over-gown from her shoulders; she felt it drop at her feet, felt the warmth of his hand through the dainty material of her nightdress. He took his mouth away at last and she inhaled over and over again.

'Yes? Leon . . . what?' He was laughing at her, laughing because of the response he had without difficulty elicited from her. 'I'm still waiting for that confession of love,' he added before she could speak.

'I love you,' she whispered, abandoned now as fire raged through her body, fire ignited by the flames of his own torrid passion. She could feel the racing beat of his heart, could feel the strong, virile hardness which had brought her arching against him over and over again while his hands had explored and his mouth had bruised. Passion had invaded her, passion in all its unsullied, primitive beauty and innocence.

She whispered close to his breast, 'When did you begin to love me?'

He held her from him, sardonic amusement in his eyes as they scanned her face, noticing the dreamy shadows as her lashes swept down, the quivering of her mouth, the blood tinting the delicate bones of her cheeks. 'So at last you believe me?'

183

'When?' she repeated. Leon gave her a warning glance and she added swiftly, 'Yes, oh, yes! I believe you!'

'And now I have to try to remember when it started?' A low laugh escaped him. 'Is it important, dearest?'

'I'd very much like to know,' she persisted, although she had no idea why she should be wasting time like this when she desired nothing more than that he should take her to bed, lie with her in the sweet intimacy of the love they had just confessed to one another.

'I wonder sometimes if it began right at the start—when I first met your eyes in that dining-room, before I even noticed the ring.'

'There were times when I felt you cared—I mean afterwards, when we were married.'

'You mean, of course, after you'd made the discovery that I'd married you for the ring?'

She nodded with a smile. 'Yes. But I was so stubborn—'

A tender finger over her lips stopped her, and Leon said gently, 'It's all in the past, love, just as the anxiety of Marina's illness is now in the past.' He was pushing the straps of her nightgown from her shoulders, his hands warm and tender against her flesh. She quivered beneath his touch, thrilling to the intimacy when, with her nightgown down to her waist, he left it there to fondle the soft skin of her breast, his lean, possessive fingers caressing the nipple before his mouth, full-lipped and moistly sensuous, closed upon it and she knew a spasm of sheer rapture as his tongue moved and manipulated until the nipple was raised to a hard bud of desire. Kathryn's body seemed out of control as it writhed and arched, with the blood surging to her heart and her temples drumming so that for the moment every other sound was blanketed out. It seemed her nerves would explode when at last he picked her up and carried her across the room, her nightgown trailing for a while before dropping to the floor a few yards from the negligee. He laid her down with such gentleness that it savoured of reverence, and she smiled happily up at him, wishing she could speak, to describe the great joy within her, the supreme contentment that enveloped her whole being.

Yet, after all, words were not necessary, she mused when presently he lay down beside her after switching off the bright ceiling light, leaving only the soft rose-peach glow of the small bed lamp. No, words were not necessary and she turned with a joyous, sensual movement to enter the sanctuary of his arms, revelling at the contact with his flesh—the hard chest whose thick black hairs were a temptation in themselves as they pressed against her breasts, the rise and fall of his stomach, the hard virility of him throbbing urgently into her thighs.

His warm, possessive hands roamed over her eager, naked form, exploring and discovering just as if it were the first time he had made love to her.

She knew instinctively that it would always be like this, new and wonderful and exciting. He found her secret places, vulnerable places, and exulted in his triumph when he heard her throaty whisper against his cheek, 'Love me, my dear husband . . . I need you so much. . . .'

He held her tenderly, though, and seemed to want to get his breath back, and allow her to get hers back, too. She thrilled to his tenderness, to the gentle way his hand closed over her lower curves while the other curled around her breast. His mouth was not idle; it closed over the other breast in sensuous and faintly arrogant possession and she sensed his intended mastery even though his every act was gentle and tender.

'Darling . . . I'm hungry for you,' he whispered in a husky bass tone . . . and he was on top of her, possessing her receptive body, transporting her to the nerve-shattering and dizzy heights of rapture, and his gift to her was the sweet prelude to his own fulfilment.

It was a long while afterwards that, his arms encircling her protectively, he said in soft and gentle tones, 'Was there anything else you had to tell me, sweetheart?'

She moved so swiftly that he thought for a moment it was another spasm of rapture, but her words told him it was only surprise that had caused her to give a start. 'What c-could there be?' she began hesitantly.

He touched one breast and said, 'I think you know what there could be,' and he drew her a little closer, without passion, just in infinite tenderness and love. 'These lovely breasts did not fill out for no reason at all.' He paused, then added with a hint of tender humour, 'You're blushing there, beneath the sheet. Come on out and let me look at you.'

But she snuggled even closer to his breast and said in

a muffled voice, 'There could be . . . be something else, dearest Leon, but I am not quite sure.'

He made no response, but merely held her close to his heart. Kathryn's arms came about him and she gave a deep contented sigh.

Once again, words were not necessary. . . .

Silhouette *Romance*

15-Day Free Trial Offer
6 Silhouette Romances

6 Silhouette Romances, free for 15 days! We'll send you 6 new Silhouette Romances to keep for 15 days, absolutely free! If you decide not to keep them, send them back to us. You pay nothing.

Free Home Delivery. But if you enjoy them as much as we think you will, keep them by paying the invoice enclosed with your free trial shipment. We'll pay all shipping and handling charges. You get the convenience of Home Delivery and we pay the postage and handling charge each month.

Don't miss a copy. The Silhouette Book Club is the way to make sure you'll be able to receive every new romance we publish before they're sold out. There is no minimum number of books to buy and you can cancel at any time.

This offer expires August 31, 1982

Silhouette Book Club, Dept. SBM 17B
120 Brighton Road, Clifton, NJ 07012

Please send me 6 Silhouette Romances to keep for 15 days, absolutely free. I understand I am not obligated to join the Silhouette Book Club unless I decide to keep them.

NAME

ADDRESS

CITY_____STATE_____ZIP_____

Silhouette Romance

IT'S YOUR OWN SPECIAL TIME

Contemporary romances for today's women.
Each month, six very special love stories will be yours
from SILHOUETTE. Look for them wherever books are sold
or order now from the coupon below.

$1.50 each

Hampson	☐ 1 ☐ 4 ☐ 16 ☐ 27 ☐ 28 ☐ 40 ☐ 52 ☐ 64 ☐ 94	Browning	☐ 12 ☐ 38 ☐ 53 ☐ 73 ☐ 93
Stanford	☐ 6 ☐ 25 ☐ 35 ☐ 46 ☐ 58 ☐ 88	Michaels	☐ 15 ☐ 32 ☐ 61 ☐ 87
		John	☐ 17 ☐ 34 ☐ 57 ☐ 85
Hastings	☐ 13 ☐ 26 ☐ 44 ☐ 67	Beckman	☐ 8 ☐ 37 ☐ 54 ☐ 72 ☐ 96
Vitek	☐ 33 ☐ 47 ☐ 66 ☐ 84		

$1.50 each

☐ 3 Powers	☐ 29 Wildman	☐ 56 Trent	☐ 79 Halldorson
☐ 5 Goforth	☐ 30 Dixon	☐ 59 Vernon	☐ 80 Stephens
☐ 7 Lewis	☐ 31 Halldorson	☐ 60 Hill	☐ 81 Roberts
☐ 9 Wilson	☐ 36 McKay	☐ 62 Hallston	☐ 82 Dailey
☐ 10 Caine	☐ 39 Sinclair	☐ 63 Brent	☐ 83 Hallston
☐ 11 Vernon	☐ 41 Owen	☐ 69 St. George	☐ 86 Adams
☐ 14 Oliver	☐ 42 Powers	☐ 70 Afton Bonds	☐ 89 James
☐ 19 Thornton	☐ 43 Robb	☐ 71 Ripy	☐ 90 Major
☐ 20 Fulford	☐ 45 Carroll	☐ 74 Trent	☐ 92 McKay
☐ 21 Richards	☐ 48 Wildman	☐ 75 Carroll	☐ 95 Wisdom
☐ 22 Stephens	☐ 49 Wisdom	☐ 76 Hardy	☐ 97 Clay
☐ 23 Edwards	☐ 50 Scott	☐ 77 Cork	☐ 98 St. George
☐ 24 Healy	☐ 55 Ladame	☐ 78 Oliver	☐ 99 Camp

$1.75 each

☐ 100 Stanford	☐ 105 Eden	☐ 110 Trent	☐ 115 John
☐ 101 Hardy	☐ 106 Dailey	☐ 111 South	☐ 116 Lindley
☐ 102 Hastings	☐ 107 Bright	☐ 112 Stanford	☐ 117 Scott
☐ 103 Cork	☐ 108 Hampson	☐ 113 Browning	☐ 118 Dailey
☐ 104 Vitek	☐ 109 Vernon	☐ 114 Michaels	☐ 119 Hampson

6 brand new Silhouette Special Editions yours for 15 days–Free!

For the reader who wants more…more story…more detail and description…more realism…and more romance…in paperback originals, 1/3 longer than our regular Silhouette Romances. Love lingers longer in new Silhouette Special Editions. Love weaves an intricate, provocative path in a third more pages than you have just enjoyed. It is love as you have always wanted it to be—and more —intriguingly depicted by your favorite Silhouette authors in the inimitable Silhouette style.

15-Day Free Trial Offer

We will send you 6 new Silhouette Special Editions to keep for 15 days absolutely free! If you decide not to keep them, send them back to us, you pay nothing. But if you enjoy them as much as we think you will, keep them and pay the invoice enclosed with your trial shipment. You will then automatically become a member of the Special Edition Book Club and receive 6 more romances every month. There is no minimum number of books to buy and you can cancel at any time.

Coming next month from
Silhouette Romances

Song of the West by Nora Roberts

Samantha couldn't say good-bye to the windswept plains of Wyoming. Had she fallen in love with the countryside, or with the commanding rancher who had corralled her heart?

Stardust by Anne Hampson

Jody quickly fell in love with her business partner, Conor Blake, but seemed destined for heartbreak when her beautiful but cruel stepsister tried to steal his heart.

A New Dawn by Ellen Goforth

Cara Logan was determined to make decorating her career until she met Mathewson Daniels, an exacting client who demanded professional *and* personal attention.

Love Captive by Jacqueline Hope

Caught in a family feud, Anne McCullough was "kidnapped" by a furious Spanish gentleman. But after spending time with her handsome captor, Anne wished the feud would never end.

Nightstar by Fern Michaels

Chosen to represent Nightstar perfume, model Caren Ainsley was thrilled when New York's cosmetics king took an interest in her. Was he striving for success in sales or love?

Renegade Player by Dixie Browning

After escaping the stifling atmosphere of her father's wealth, Willemena reveled in her freedom. But her frivolous life-style might cost her the only man she'd ever loved.

**Look for *Wildcatter's Woman* by Janet Dailey
Available in May.**